DESIRE OF MY

HEART

a novel

Kathryn, May you always follow the Lord Shepherd and be receptive of His fellowship.

Clytee C. Dugan
Psalm 37:4

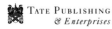

TATE PUBLISHING
& Enterprises

Tate Publishing is committed to excellence in the publishing industry. Our staff of highly trained professionals, including editors, graphic designers, and marketing personnel, work together to produce the very finest books available. The company reflects the philosophy established by the founders, based on Psalms 68:11,

"THE LORD GAVE THE WORD AND GREAT WAS THE COMPANY OF THOSE WHO PUBLISHED IT."

If you would like further information, please contact us:

1.888.361.9473 | www.tatepublishing.com

TATE PUBLISHING *& Enterprises*, LLC | 127 E. Trade Center Terrace
Mustang, Oklahoma 73064 USA

Desire of My Heart

Scripture quotations are taken from the Holy Bible, King James Version, Cambridge, 1769. Used by permission. All rights reserved.

This novel is a work of fiction. Names, descriptions, entities and incidents included in the story are products of the author's imagination. Any resemblance to actual persons, events and entities is entirely coincidental.

Published in the United States of America

ISBN: 978-1-5988661-7-9

07.01.25

DESIRE OF MY
HEART

a novel

C.C. DUZAN

Tate Publishing & Enterprises

Dedication

God gave me the story. Therefore, I dedicate this endeavor to him that it shall not return unto him void, but it shall accomplish that which he pleases (Isaiah 55:11).

Acknowledgment

With a grateful heart, I express my appreciation to my son Stephen, to my nephew Daniel, and to my daughter Jennifer, whose computer expertise made this project possible. Thank you, family and friends, for your prayers and encouragement.

Genealogy of Characters

Clara Cook (1880-1941) married in
    1900 to Egbert Wirth (1870-1939)

Hester Wirth (1904-   )

Lena Cook (1885-   ) married in 1910
    to William Clifton (1875-1937)

Amy Louise Clifton (1915-1944) married in
    1938 to Charles Anderson (1914-   )

Laura Ruth Clifton (1918-   ) married in
    1941 to John Greely (1917-Dec. 7, 1941)

Karl de Kort (1890- ?) married in 1910
    to Ingrid Wagenlied (1892-1937)

Alfred de Kort (1912-   ) married in
    1935 to Rosalie Dunning (1914-   )

Karl de Kort (1939-   )

Gretchen de Kort (1915-   )

PART I
Middleton, Missouri
1964

Chapter 1

College was over!

Like water spraying from a shower head, the students came out all doors of the dormitories laden with clothes, boxes, shoes, and mementos of dorm life. With fragmented conversations, a hug, and some tears, they stuffed their many possessions into the waiting vehicles, gave a final wave of the hand, and drove away, leaving the buildings filled with silence and empty rooms

As if viewing a movie without sound, Nellie Dunkirk watched this activity from a second floor window of Mrs. Murphy's boarding house. Before the commencement exercises last evening, she had also been a member of the Middleton College student body, though not as much a part as if she had lived in a dorm.

Instead, Nellie lived in the boarding house, and though it was just across the street from the campus, it still wasn't the same. Nellie had never been included in any pajama parties, gab sessions, or test-crammings, though she knew such things took place. She had overheard talk in the library and had read the gossip columns in the student newspaper. But the social life on campus had not been for her. Nellie had attended Middleton College for the academic studies and had worked in the library to help pay her way. She had regarded herself as singular, an outsider, alone.

But today, Nellie felt different.

True, she still lived in Mrs. Murphy's boarding house. The same dotted Swiss curtains still framed the single window of her room as they had last year (and many years before). The same patchwork coverlet was spread over the bed she had slept in alone these past four years. Yes, outwardly, everything appeared the same.

Yet Nellie was not the same. That day she was a 1964 graduate of Middleton College, an employed member of society, and an adult. She felt "grown-up," mature, prepared to face the world, and in control of her schedule.

As she stood gazing out the window, Nellie wondered just where she would now be if she had accepted Rodney Blake's proposal of marriage three years before.

"Let's get married," he had pled. "What difference does it make about your name? You're Nellie Dunkirk to me. Just forget all that other stuff."

"It isn't that easy, Rod," she had tried to explain. "I can't pass over nineteen years pretending they didn't happen. Who am I? Who are my parents? Why was I out in a snowstorm alone? There must be some explanation, and I want to know it!"

"That's not important to me. I've been offered a job in Tulsa. I had hoped you'd go with me. We seem to hit it off pretty good. But if you'd rather chase butterflies than marry me, then go chase your butterflies!" And Rodney Blake had left in a huff.

Not once, Nellie reflected, had he said anything about his loving her. Not once had he offered to hold her or kiss her. Maybe he did have a job in Tulsa. Somehow she doubted it. He'd not keep it. Rod did not stick to anything very long. That's why he had quit college after one year.

Moving from job to job was an old story to Nellie. She had had enough of that. Until they came to Middleton eight years before, Mama and Nellie had lived in a lot of places.

As long as she could remember, Nellie had been known as "Greta's Girl." A hotel, a club, a restaurant—the kitchens were different, yet similar. After all, a kitchen is a kitchen. Nellie had refrained from hanging around where Mama worked. She felt in the way—and was sometimes told to go elsewhere. She was so grateful for libraries. She preferred to spend her free time where she could sit and read. She felt more at ease among books.

Then one day she would return to their room to find the cardboard suitcase opened on the bed. Moving again! Putting their few belongings in the suitcase and Greta's black valise, they would board another bus.

Mama always found work. Appearing in a club or hotel kitchen, she would announce to the one in charge that she was a bread and pastry cook. "No pay, first day. After that, you pay," she'd explain. With his permission, she would make some delectable pastry that would "sell" her skills to the management. She would have employment then—until someone became too curious about her or Nellie. Questions about their background seemed to frighten Greta. Then they'd drift to another town and another rooming house. Greta would go to another kitchen and Nellie to another library.

Greta had always seen to it that Nellie had plenty to eat, proper clothes to wear, and that she was clean. Never had Nellie doubted Greta's care for her. Not having a Daddy had not bothered her either. Other children in her room at school had lost their dads during World War II. She just assumed the same for herself. Greta was "Mama" to her, and that was sufficient. Not until she reached adolescence did she learn Greta was not her real mother.

When Nellie had questioned Greta about her birth, Greta had said, "You snow baby. I find you crying. I care for you."

As time moved them further from WW II, Greta and Nellie would stay longer in a town. Eight years before, they had come to Middleton, Missouri. Nellie had been grateful for a larger high school where she could blend in—to be just one more face in the student body. She had no desire for any personal attention to be focused on her. She was too shy for that.

Mrs. Murphy's boarding house in Middleton was near the high school and just across the street from the college campus. Greta had worked at the Oak Hills Country Club while Nellie attended high school. Then in June, after Nellie's graduation, Greta had packed her black valise and boarded an outbound bus. That was four years ago, and Nellie had not seen nor heard from Greta.

Rodney Blake had been Nellie's friend then. No doubt, Greta thought she and Rodney would one day marry and operate the Blake Grocery Store. But it had not worked out that way.

At first, Nellie had missed Rodney's happy-go-lucky companionship. She knew in her heart, however, that she had not loved him with the kind of devotion necessary for marriage. No tears, no regrets, and no broken promises, she had decided.

Nellie turned from the window and continued dressing. The gathered skirt of her sleeveless summer dress emphasized her slender figure just as the leaves of the floral print brought out the color of her green eyes. For a moment she stared at her reflection in the oval mirror above the pine dresser. Then, pulling a comb through her shoulder-length brown hair, she parted off one portion, draped it to one side, and pinned the wave above her left ear. She was pleased with the effect—and herself. She was glad she had stayed in college. With her degree in library science, she was confident she could always find work. At the moment, she was glad to have a job at the college library.

She felt independent that day. She felt free—free to do something she wanted to do. No longer was she controlled by classroom bells.

TODAY—this very day—she would begin her search to discover her name. Picking up her purse and the novel she was returning to the library, Nellie walked out of her room and resolutely down the stairs.

Chapter 2

A few moments later, Nellie was standing at the sideboard in the dining room of Mrs. Murphy's boarding house. She half-filled a bowl with breakfast flakes and generously spooned in home-canned peaches before adding cream. She put a small patty of butter on her plate and added a spoonful of plum jelly made from the fruit of the tree in the Murphy's back yard. She was savoring the aroma of toasting bread when a male voice behind her stated: "Ummmm, that smells good enough to eat!"

"Oh, it is!" agreed Nellie, turning to face the voice. The young man inside the door was positively the most handsome she had ever seen. From his blond hair to the toes of his shining shoes, he was as beautiful as Adonis himself. Nellie's pulse raced. She was sure he could hear her pounding heart. With extreme effort she was able to say, "It's some of Mrs. Murphy's homemade light bread. She bakes every Friday to have it fresh for Saturday's brunch. And it tastes as good as it smells!" she finished breathlessly. She indicated for the young man to help himself to the fare on the sideboard.

"I'm Karl de Kort," he said, introducing himself, "and you must be Nellie Dunkirk. May I join you?"

"I'd be pleased, Mr. de Kort. I had heard that the new music teacher was to be a new boarder, but I didn't expect him to be so..."

"Young? No white hair? No beard?" He grinned. "I'm not the stereotypical music professor. I don't even feel like a teacher yet. Have you lived here long?" he inquired.

"Eight years—while I attended high school and Middleton College," she replied.

"Then you are not a student," he stated. Surveying the laden sideboard, he added, "Breakfast in Vienna wasn't like this!"

"Nor at Mrs. Murphy's except on Saturdays," said Nellie. "She calls this brunch, a combination of breakfast and lunch. That's why there's such a variety."

"An early lunch like this makes for a longer afternoon, doesn't it?" he asked, looking at Nellie with a questioning look on his face. "I suppose you already have something planned for today?"

"Well, yes. I'm taking this book to the library and..."

"Are you a Faulkner fan?" he asked, picking up the copy of *The Reivers*.

"Not exactly, though I have read several of his books. I chose this one because Faulkner was given the Pulitzer Prize for it last year. Do you do much reading?" she asked.

"Not as much as I'd like. Much of my time is spent at the keyboard. Though I did read *Intruder in the Dust* for a course I had in college," he hastened to add.

"Where did you go to college, Mr. de Kort?" asked Nellie, making conversation.

"Right here at Middleton. And, please, call me Karl. I'm not that much older than you," he said.

"You did!" Nellie was surprised. "Why, I understood that you were from Pennsylvania."

"I am. At least, that's my home address. But my mother's grandfather was T.T. Dunning, the founder of the music department here at Middleton. When I showed interest in music for a career, my mother wanted me to come here to school. So, I lived with Grandmother Dunning and attended college here."

As they ate and talked, Nellie studied Karl de Kort as she had many other persons who had sat in a library in her line of view. At ease among strangers, this man seemed capable of conversing in an interesting manner with anyone. As he talked, he made gestures—not meaningless flutterings of his hands, but graceful movements that added punctuation to his words.

Often, a smile played about his lips and added a sparkle to his gray eyes. At times, the smile was more a boyish grin. Norman Rockwell could have added a splash of freckles to that nose, put a can of worms and a fishing pole in those hands, and sold the canvas for thousands of dollars, she mused.

Nellie was charmed by his blond good looks, though Karl appeared to be unknowledgeable of his handsomeness. He spoke with appreciation for the support given to him by his parents and grandparents.

There was silence.

Nellie realized he was waiting for her to reply to his question. "I'm sorry," she apologized, looking down at her plate while a flush swept across her face. "I did not hear what you said."

"You didn't finish what you started to say about your plans for today," he reminded her.

Embarrassed, Nellie felt herself blushing again. "Oh, I'm going to the library to do some research on a matter I've wanted to do for a long time."

"I hope you don't think I'm hasty, for I know we've just

met, but would you have time to take a drive with me later on this afternoon? This is such a beautiful day and—"

"That sounds lovely!" interrupted Nellie. "It's been a long time since I've been on a drive. Attending classes, working at the library, and studying in my room has been my routine for months and months. A drive sounds very inviting." She rose to stack her dishes on the wheeled cart by the kitchen door.

"That's settled then," he said, adding his dishes to the cart. "You do what you want to do at the library, and I'll go to my office. I still have books to unpack and other stuff to put in place." He looked at his watch and added, "I'll come to the library for you, say, 3:30, okay?"

"I'll be ready. Thank you for asking me."

Chapter 3

At 3:25, Nellie was waiting just inside the main entrance of Greenfield Hall, more commonly known as the library. From there she could see the driveway that meandered through the campus. As she watched for Karl de Kort, Nellie realized she did not have any idea what kind of car he had.

One vehicle after another paraded by her viewing stand. One car, a pale green Falcon, pulled over to the curb and stopped. Seeing Karl emerge from the driver's side, Nellie pushed open the heavy glass door and met him on the portico of the building.

"Warmed up some, didn't it?" he greeted her with a smile.

"Yes, but it's still a beautiful day," she agreed, tossing her head to let the breeze lift her hair.

"No faster than I'll be driving, we can leave the windows down," he said as he held the door for her to slide into the front seat.

Nellie pulled a babushka from her purse, flipped it over her head, and tied it under her chin. "Let the breezes blow," she laughed. "I'm ready." She was very conscious of Karl's presence and the scent of his after shave. The interior of the car broadcast its male owner. She had to mentally force herself to relax, to breathe naturally, and swallow her pulse.

Meanwhile, Karl had steered the car away from the campus. Soon Nellie was in a part of Middleton she had never seen before. Ancient trees lined the streets and spread their cool shade over the wide front yards. The houses, sitting back from the street, were large and quite ornate.

Slowing the car, Karl entered a narrow driveway. "This is the Dunning place," he announced. He stopped the car just inside the entrance and switched off the engine. "When my great-grandfather built this house just before the turn of the century, these were dirt streets, and folks rode in horse-drawn carriages. The story in the family is that Great-grandma Kate insisted the house be far enough from the road that the dust would not reach her parlor. Her precious pump organ and the lace curtains she had bought in St. Louis on her honeymoon were in the parlor," he said, mimicking a fastidious old lady.

Laughing, Nellie turned to look at "the Dunning place." She saw a large, two-story white frame house set on a rise over-looking the front yard. Dozens and dozens of white spindles formed a balustrade outlining a veranda that stretched across the wide front and halfway down the near side of the house. More spindles framed a false balcony above a huge bay window. Lattice work and ornamentation decorated each gable. At the apex of the roof was a cupola with a weathervane on top. Panes of stained glass added color above each front window and on either side of the massive front door.

"The house, the yard—they are so big! Why it must take hours to cut the grass and gallons of paint to cover all that gingerbread!" exclaimed Nellie.

"I can't vouch for the paint, but I can for the lawn mowing. That started out being one of my chores when I lived with Grandmother Dunning. By the time I'd get it all cut, it would be time to start again. I couldn't do it and keep up with my piano practice. So Grandmother finally had to hire it done."

Karl pointed out the car window. "All this land, even farther than that new overpass, was all Dunning land over a hundred years ago. My mother's father was the only son and fell heir to the house. The rest of the farm was divided between his sisters. Much has since been sold out of the family. New houses now stand where the Dunning mule barns and hay fields once were."

Karl paused.

"Go on," urged Nellie.

"I really hated to not be here for Grandmother's funeral last year. She and I knew when I left to go to Vienna that she might not be here when I returned. I rather dreaded the first time back here alone. That's why I decided to ask you to come with me. You seemed to be someone who might understand."

"I'm glad you asked me. Is there more you want to tell me? I find this all very interesting," said Nellie.

"The house is just as Grandmother left it. My mother will be coming to Missouri in August when the estate is to be settled. It's been a good name, Dunning. But the family is about to die out," Karl explained. "My mother had only one brother. He was still single when he was killed during World War II. I am the only immediate male descendant, and my name isn't Dunning. That's almost sad, isn't it?"

"Yes, I suppose it is. You, at least, know who you are. You have a family..." Nellie choked on the words. Although she clenched her teeth and tightly closed her eyes, the tears still escaped.

Seeing a girl cry was a new experience for Karl. He did not know what to do or say. Once he reached out a hand as if to touch the girl, then he pulled it back.

Regaining her composure, Nellie was quick to apologize. "I'm sorry. Maybe I am being selfish, or just jealous. You see, at the commencement exercises last evening, President Richardson asked the parents to stand while their graduate walked across the stage to receive his or her degree. Of all those graduates, I was probably the only one who walked 'alone.' I don't have..." Nellie turned her head to keep Karl from seeing the new tears forming in her eyes.

"I'm sorry, too," sympathized Karl. "Too bad your parents couldn't be here to see you graduate."

"That's not it! That's not it at all!" she corrected him. "It's not that they couldn't be here. I don't even know my parents."

"You what?" exclaimed Karl in disbelief.

"Ironic, isn't it? You lament the loss of a family name when I don't even know my name!"

"You don't?" Karl was shocked by that statement.

"It's true. I was brought up by a woman who heard a child crying and found me in a snow bank one November night in 1944. She guessed me to be about two at that time."

"Well, I never!" Karl interjected while offering Nellie his handkerchief.

Drying her eyes, Nellie continued, "Mrs. Murphy is always talking about a bowl, a piece of Irish lace, or a 'raceet' from the 'auld country.' How many times I've wished for a pair of baby shoes, a photo, a lock of hair, anything—even a tombstone that would be a tie to show I belong to someone, that I am part of a family." Turning to face Karl, Nellie added, "I shouldn't have unloaded on you like this. I'm truly sorry. My feelings are not your responsibility."

"That's okay, really," Karl was quick to reply. "You probably needed a good cry. At least I know more about you than I did."

"That's for sure," agreed Nellie. "Before I interrupted you with my tears, you were telling me about your mother's family. Do go on, please."

"Are you sure you're all right?" asked Karl.

"Yes, I'm fine," Nellie answered with a weak smile. "I won't cry anymore, I promise. And I do want to hear more."

"Well, my mother's father—that was Granddad Earl Dunning—promised her as a graduation gift that she could have a year's study in Vienna with the organ master Karl de Kort. That's my other grandfather, not me. While in Vienna, Mother met Alfred de Kort and his sister Gretchen. They became very good friends. In fact, Alfred followed my mother back to the United States in 1936 to court and marry her."

"What an interesting story!" exclaimed Nellie. "So romantic!"

"It doesn't end there. Since Hitler was taking over Europe, my parents invited Grandfather de Kort and Aunt Gretchen to come to the United States. Grandfather chose not to leave his homeland, but Aunt Gretchen did come in 1938. At first she was content to just visit with them. Then she desired to work. My father claims that his sister had a beautiful singing voice. She was studying opera in Vienna. Anyway, she auditioned for and was accepted by an opera company that was touring our country. When I was born, Mother mailed Aunt Gretchen a birth announcement, but it was returned unclaimed. She had moved without leaving a forwarding address. My family still doesn't know her whereabouts. She just seems to have disappeared."

"How awful!"

"After the war, my father tried again to locate Aunt

Gretchen and his father. We assume that Grandfather de Kort died during World War II. We still have nothing to prove if Aunt Gretchen is alive, either."

"Don't give up hope," Nellie encouraged. "If you have no proof she is dead, she must be alive. Maybe she is living under an assumed name somewhere. Just keep hoping. That's all I have—hope. I want so much to learn who I am. Some day, I hope to find my family."

"How do you propose to do that?" Karl wanted to know.

"I started today. That's the research I mentioned to you earlier. I'm viewing the microfilms of the newspapers we have in the library for November, 1944. Somewhere there is a family who lost a little girl. You've no way of knowing how I yearn for a family and to have my own name. I am so tired of being 'Greta's girl'!"

"Greta's girl! What do you mean by that?" asked Karl.

Leaning back in the car seat, Nellie watched the breeze stir the leaves of an aged maple as she talked. She told Karl things she'd never told anyone before. How effortless it was to talk with him. Time passed as she related her story.. She felt as if she'd known him for years. At last she told about coming to Middleton.

"Where's Greta now?" he asked.

"I don't know. I haven't seen her since the June after I finished high school. She knew I had a job at the college library and that I was planning to get a degree in library science. She probably thought that Rodney Blake and I—Rod was the boy I dated some—would one day be married and take over the Blake Grocery Store. Anyway, she left, and I've not seen or heard a word from her."

"Why did this Greta just grab you out of the weather and run off? Why didn't she take you to the police station? The police might have located your family. She sounds a little suspicious to me."

"I really don't know. Lately I've wondered that myself. In 1944, though, the United States and Germany were at war, remember? She must have had a reason, in her way of thinking."

"Are you saying she's German? Greta is a German name, but Dunkirk is not. Did she tell you she was German?"

"I really don't remember. Mama never spoke German. In fact, Mama didn't talk much. She did sing in German, however. Oftentimes, she would sing when she was taking down her braids to brush her long blonde hair. I remember so well one song she often sang. It went like this," and Nellie hummed a few bars.

"I know that!" exclaimed Karl. "That's the 'Children's Prayer' from Humperdinck's opera '*Hansel and Gretel*.' Opera. Say, do you have a picture of your mama?"

"Just a dime store picture is all. It's not very good. Both of us crowded into the booth, and Mama had to crouch down behind me for the picture." Producing the well-worn photo, Nellie gave it to Karl, adding, "See, about all you can tell about Mama is she wore her braids around her head. Karl, you don't think that Mama is your Aunt Gretchen?" asked Nellie excitedly.

"I've thought of that. Wouldn't that be a coincidence!"

"The names Greta and Gretchen are very similar," stated Nellie thoughtfully.

"Yes, they are," agreed Karl. "And if you say de Kort just so, it can almost sound like Dunkirk, too."

"But why would she change her name," asked Nellie, "assuming the two persons were the same?"

"That I do not know." Karl studied the picture intently

then returned it to Nellie. "You're right. I can't tell much about her. I've never seen Aunt Gretchen, or even a picture of her. I'd have no way to recognize her if I were to see her. She doesn't even know that I exist. The only thing in my favor is I do bear her father's name."

"I'd think that would demand a reaction from her if you'd ever meet. But that would be a real happenstance, for sure. If I knew where Mama was, we could ask her. But I don't know."

"Back to your research this afternoon. Did you find any thing at all?" inquired Karl.

"I don't know if I did or not. I learned there was a train accident in St. Louis about 11:30 PM on November 28, 1944. It involved a troop train, and eighteen persons were killed . I'm not able to make a connection between a small child and a troop train, however."

"There might be," Karl said. "Did you learn what caused the accident?"

"No, I ran out of time. I had to stop in order to meet you at 3:30. I'll have to locate that paper again and—"

"Let's go look now!" Karl suggested excitedly. "Is the college library still the public library for the county?"

"Yes."

"Good! Then it's still open, even if it is Saturday. Let's go!" He started the engine and backed the car out of the Dunning driveway.

Inside Greenfield Hall, Nellie led the way into the research area, located the microfilm of the St. Louis Post-Dispatch, and flashed the article on the viewer.

EIGHTEEN KILLED IN TRAIN
ACCIDENT IN ST. LOUIS
Weather Affects Visibility

Eighteen persons were killed last night in St. Louis when a troop train hit the last car of the Eastern Flyer. The Flyer, a passenger train headed for Chicago and points East, had pulled onto a siding to allow a troop train to pass. The last car of the crowded passenger train was not completely off the main line and due to blizzard conditions, the engineer of the troop train was unable to see the lights on the standing train. The accident occurred at approximately 11:30 PM

"How awful!" shuddered Nellie. "There's nothing said about a missing child, though."

"No, but there was a blizzard. You said Greta found you in a snow storm about midnight."

"This accident was about 11:30 PM, so that fits," she agreed.

"And one was a passenger train. So that's where the child could have come from," explained Karl.

"Let's see what else we can learn," said Nellie as she flashed the next issue on the viewer.

Methodically they viewed both St. Louis daily newspapers. When Professor Spencer blinked the lights to signal closing time for the library, Nellie and Karl had not discovered anything more.

A whole new influx of students filled the dormitories and invaded the library when summer school began on Monday.

Nellie soon learned that being a full-time librarian was quite different from being a student helper who sandwiched working hours in between classes. She worked two four-hour blocks each day—the morning, the afternoon, or the night block. When the day was over, Nellie was tired! Yet she enjoyed the activity and gained personal satisfaction in believing her labors were beneficial.

Some who came to the library were like Agnes. A school teacher taking some refresher courses, Agnes explained to Nellie, "Our school library is a table in the English room where we keep the books we get each month off the Bookmobile. Our only file is homemade from a recipe box and index cards. I know I sound backwoodsy, but would you help me? Prof. Ficklin insists we study the characterization techniques of Ben Ames Williams in his short story entitled, 'They Grind Exceedingly Small.' I don't have the slightest idea how to find it."

And then there was Dudley. He knew his way around in a library. He would gather what resource materials he needed, go into one of the private study rooms behind the stacks, and lose himself in concentration. The first night Nellie was responsible for lock-up, she almost locked Dudley in the building. She had blinked the lights as Professor Spencer had indicated in ample time for everyone to leave, she thought. But Dudley had fallen asleep, thereby missing the signal. When she made her last circuit checking that the lights were off in the restrooms, she happened to see a sliver of light shining under the door of the study room. That saved him from a lonely, all-night vigil in the empty building.

During some of her off hours, Nellie used that time to sit at the microfilm reader to view old newspapers. Hour after hour, she checked the events and happenings of twenty years ago but found nothing to assist her in her search.

Karl continued to encourage her. "Keep on looking and hoping. Don't give up," he would say. At times, she was discouraged, but his prodding compelled her to continue.

Together, Karl and Nellie attended staff activities, went for long walks, sat in Mrs. Murphy's porch swing, and talked and talked. The more they were together, the more they seemed to enjoy being together and hated to be apart. Karl would drop by the library "just to see you," and she frequently watched him at practice. He would be so engrossed in his music that he would not be aware that she had slipped inside the recital hall.

Sitting in the last row of the darkened auditorium, she would watch him practice on the concert grand on stage. Just sitting there and watching, Nellie began to recognize the discipline, determination, and preparation necessary for Karl to be a classical pianist. Over and over he would drill on some portion. When he finally laid aside the musical score, Nellie could almost sense Karl's very being oozing out of his fingertips. His music was such a joy to her that she hated to have to leave when her time was up.

Nellie was thrilled with anticipation when Karl announced his piano concert.

"When?" asked Nellie.

"The first Friday in August," he replied. "It seems to be a tradition here for a new member of the music faculty to perform during his first term. I'm brushing up my repertoire I presented at the Vienna Conservatory last spring."

"I can hardly wait!" she sighed.

"Deliberately changing the subject, Karl asked, "Do you know what Saturday is?"

"It's the Fourth of July. Why?"

"Let's have a picnic, just the two of us," he said, letting his eyes linger on the curve of her lips.

"Sounds like fun!" Nellie replied, admonishing herself to be careful

Chapter 5

July, 1964

On Saturday, Nellie wore a white sleeveless blouse with the navy shorts she had been required to have for physical education class. Thinking she needed something red, she plaited her hair and tied a bright red ribbon on each braid.

Karl didn't appear as patriotic, but he did wear blue jeans and looked dressed for a picnic.

"Hey, Teach," she teased, "you don't look like a college professor in those jeans."

"Good," was his only reply.

On the outskirts of town, Karl parked the car where a bridge crossed a little stream. He carried the picnic basket, and Nellie had the blanket from the back seat. Hand in hand, they followed the brook downstream. Rocks, sticks, and tree roots obstructed its path, but the little creek babbled and gurgled on its way.

"See," Karl observed to Nellie, "like this brook, you may encounter obstructions, but accept them as part of life and go on your way. Keep your goal before you and keep on searching."

"My, what philosophy!" she teased. "And I thought you were a music teacher."

"Which reminds me," he said, shifting the subject from

himself. "Have you heard any of the songs by that group from England?"

"I guess not. Who do you mean?" she asked.

"They call themselves The Beatles. They are becoming very popular in the United States, I hear."

"Oh, I know whom you mean, now. I saw their pictures on a magazine in the library. But I've never heard them. I don't have a radio, you know," she added.

"Richard Klingner, the vocal music professor, has a record player in his studio. He invited me in to hear them. It was really strange, Nellie. I sat there listening to their screaming and thumping, and I seemed to see half-naked African natives dancing to drums in their village. Then I envisioned American Indians circling a campfire. The men seemed to use the rhythm of the drums and the noise they themselves were making to provide stimuli for what they would do next. The music—if you could call it that—seemed to bring forth their animalistic instincts, giving them the nerve to fight and destroy. In contrast, Nellie, I thought of our forefathers who danced the stately minuet or glided across the floor in a lilting waltz. They wore their very best clothes, their good manners, and conducted themselves as civilized ladies and gentlemen, while those others behaved as savages aroused to a frenzy of activity. I'm just wondering, Nellie, what will be the result if this type of music were to monopolize our American youth? Would we develop Cochises or Washingtons? This new rhythm is not the soothing music of the classics! I'll stay with them! They're my style. Say, here is a nice place."

Rounding a bend in the creek, Karl and Nellie entered a grassy area under a large cottonwood tree. After Karl spread out the blanket, Nellie opened the hamper. An item in the newspaper laid across the top caught her eye.

"What's the matter, Nellie?" asked Karl.

"Read this," she said, giving him the paper and pointing to a small paragraph under the court heading.

"BLAKE, Rodney Glenn, age 22, DWI. Held for felonious assault, possession of illegal contraband, and carrying a concealed weapon."

"Whew! I wouldn't want to be in his shoes! Who is he? Someone you know?" asked Karl.

"That's the guy that asked me to marry him three years ago," answered Nellie.

"Really?" After a pause, Karl asked, "Would you like to tell me about him?"

"No, no need." Then changing her mind, Nellie said, "Yes, I believe I will."

"I met Rodney Blake early in my third year of high school. He dashed into the library, needing some background information on a Lit assignment. I happened to be on duty that day, so I helped him to find what he needed. He returned a few days later, saying he needed a date for a line party and asked me to go with him. I had been to a few shows but I had never been out with a boy before. I agreed to go. The movie was a Walt Disney film about prairie animals. It was interesting, but the cartoon was hilarious. I remember having a lot of fun laughing at that cat and mouse, Tom and Jerry. Rod asked me again for a date, and I accepted. He was a lot of fun to be with.

"Soon, we were going out every Friday or Saturday night to the show. When basketball season started, we'd just go to the drug store for a Coke, as a show made him out too late during training. Sometimes, we would spend the evening in the Blake apartment above their grocery store.

"I thoroughly enjoyed being in Rod's home. His mother

helped in the store, but she still made their apartment seem like a real home, a place where a real family lived. She had African violets in the front windows and a bright red geranium in the kitchen. Often, she would have fresh-baked banana bread to offer us. Rod was not a basketball star, just another man on the team. I've often wondered if he would have even been that if I had not known where to obtain the information he needed to keep his grades up. Rod would rather tinker with an old car than study. Doing any kind of research was not his choice of an after-school activity.

"Yet, he was lots of fun. I enjoyed the senseless malarkey we shared. Like a habit, we continued dating when we changed from high school to college. But Rod lasted only one year. He was too busy experiencing the 'extra' to prepare himself for the 'curriculum.' His grades hit rock bottom. That's when he asked me to marry him and go to Tulsa. He never said he loved me, made no mention of romance. He said we 'hit it off pretty good,' as if a marriage was one long, good-time date.

"Looking back, I can see that Rod used me. He used me in high school to keep him on the team. He would have used me in marriage to work and supply the income. That's just not my idea of marriage. I want a home, an anchor; a man who is stable and secure."

As Nellie talked, she was setting out the picnic lunch—the sandwiches, pickles, deviled eggs, and lemonade. Karl, leaning against the cottonwood, just watched and listened. He studied the arch of her neck, on display today as she had braided her hair. When she turned, he saw for the first time a dark mole just below her left ear. Not a fast worker, he mused, but a thorough one, very neat and efficient. Hearing his name, he gave her his complete attention.

"You're not like that, Karl," she was saying. "You want to

touch, to feel, to smell, to taste every day and everything. You make each detail seem important, meaningful. I've watched you drink coffee a sip at a time, holding the cup with both hands as if it were priceless, each taste to be savored to its fullest flavor."

"That's my life, Nellie. Measure by measure, each added to the next to make a melody, a beautiful refrain. If it has no purpose, why include it? Music is practice, discipline, work. When I work, I work hard with only one purpose in mind—to obtain my goal. When I relax, I try to enjoy each moment to the fullest."

"Poor Rod. He was like a piece of driftwood tossed about in the current; no goals, no ambitions, no backbone. Anything for a good time," lamented Nellie. "Good time. That's an idea. This is supposed to be a picnic," she said as she broke off a foxtail and began to tickle Karl's nose.

"You want to play?" he asked as he pulled off Nellie's shoes. Grabbing her up in his arms, he poked her bare feet into the cold water of the creek.

Squealing and laughing, Nellie squirmed out of his arms. Reaching for a handful of water, she splashed it into Karl's face.

"Recess is over," said Karl. "Time to eat." He suddenly turned and walked back to the picnic blanket. Nellie could still feel the pressure of his arms about her, warm and exciting, an emotion somewhere between wonder and fear.

After they had eaten, Nellie gathered up what was left while Karl stretched out on the blanket to relax. .His eyes closed. Finishing her task, Nellie took a book from her purse. She leaned against the tree and began to read.. Nature's sounds were harmonious with the setting: the babbling brook, a singing bird, a buzzing bee, even the rustling leaves of the cottonwood tree. When she looked up from her book, Karl was gazing at her. She did not know how long he had been awake, but she felt the need to break the spell cast by those gray eyes. She could feel the goose bumps returning.

He made no move but seemed content to lie where he was. Propping himself on one elbow, Karl said, "I appreciate your telling me about Rodney. I can't tell you about any former girlfriends because you are the only girl I've ever dated. I had no time for girls when I was in school. My time was spent practicing piano. Then, when I did have the time, I was shy about asking. Anyway, I just practiced and practiced piano and pretended girls did not exist, until I met you."

Rising from the pallet, Karl pulled Nellie to her feet and into his arms. "I want you to be my girl, Nellie. No, don't interrupt," he said, placing his forefinger across her lips. "I know you don't feel ready to give yourself to me—or anyone. I sense your reluctance. But I don't care what your name is. You are everything I want, and that's enough for me. You have all the attributes I want in my wife. Besides, I think you have the most beautiful green eyes in the world. I really care for you, Nellie, just as you are."

Their kiss was as natural as breathing itself. The pressure of his lips on hers was tender, gentle, yet firm. It aroused feelings she had never felt before. She was aware of him, the strength of his arms and the pressure of his lips. She didn't want the kiss to end She was also aware of her own body's reaction to his nearness and the flash of warmth that enveloped her in an instant.

He released her slowly, allowing his hands to brush her shoulders and bare arms. He held her hands looking into her eyes. Right behind his touch came the sparklers, sizzling and tingling, melting all of her resistance. She felt herself drowning in his gray eyes and thought he was going to kiss her again.

Instead, he dropped her hands, saying, "We'd better go," and he quickly rolled up the blanket.

ex **Chapter 6** *ex*

Nellie was busy at the vertical file on Friday when she heard a cough behind her. Turning, she faced Karl. Shafts of light from the skylight above him accented his blond hair into a halo, but the sparkle in his eyes was anything but angelic.

Bowing low over her hand he asked, "Miss Dunkirk, may I have the pleasure of your company at dinner tonight?"

"Yes, of course, sir," she laughed. "Is this a special occasion? How should I dress?"

"I need companionship, good food, soft light, conversation, but no music. I've been practicing for hours on Beethoven's '*Pathetique*,' and I need a change. Wear whatever you wish. I'll have my limousine in front of your domicile at seven sharp."

That evening, when Karl pulled into the parking lot of a restaurant named "The Tiger," Nellie remarked, "I don't remember seeing this place before. Is it new?"

"Yes and no," answered Karl. "There was a cafe here, but the new owner has added to the building and enlarged the parking lot. Looks nice, doesn't it?"

Inside, Nellie and Karl came face to face with tigers. The huge cats were sitting, running, or crouched to leap. What made the paintings so outstanding were the cats' eyes. They literally glowed!

"I get it!" exclaimed Nellie. "The tiger is the mascot for Middleton High School, remember?"

"Of course," agreed Karl. "I remember seeing big black and orange tigers on display on the square downtown every time Middleton had a home game."

After they were settled in a corner booth and had given their order, Nellie leaned over to ask Karl. "Is there something wrong with me? That woman at the cash register hasn't taken her eyes off me since we came in. She's beginning to make me feel uneasy."

"You look beautiful to me," Karl said, taking her hand into his own. "I like you in green; really sets off your eyes."

Nellie felt herself turning pink. She was saved from comment by the waitress bringing their silverware and salads.

Karl squeezed her hand then released it. "You need not turn around, but that woman is still looking this way."

Later, when Karl went to pay their bill, the woman behind the cash register spoke to Nellie. "Excuse me, Miss. You look very much like a woman I once knew that I was wondering if you might be her daughter. Is your name Greely?"

"Why, no, it isn't," replied Nellie.

"You certainly look like Mrs. Greely did back in the Forties. She had a little girl then that would be about your age now. Sorry to have bothered you." Punching the keys of the cash register, she counted out Karl's change.

"Oh, you haven't bothered me!" Nellie was quick to reply. "Tell me more about your friend. I'm really quite interested."

"Really not much to tell," the woman explained. "I went to school in the city. An old man—we called him Pop Jenkins—ran the Forum. That was an ice cream parlor on Washington Avenue down from the Regal Theater. Pop kept the Forum open late on Fridays and Saturdays to give the kids a place to hang out after the show. This Mrs. Greely worked for Pop. Sometimes when I'd stop for an ice cream cone after school, Mrs. Greely's little girl would be there, too. You certainly look like Mrs. Greely."

"I'm sorry to disappoint you, but I'm not aware that I've any relatives with that name. It's an interesting story, though. Thank you for telling it to me. May I ask you a question?"

"Of course."

"Where did you get these beautiful tiger paintings?" asked Nellie. "Their eyes simply glow!"

"I painted them myself—on black velvet. I'm glad you like them. Their eyes are glass beads. I looked and looked before I found the kind I wanted. Here, let me show you the Tiger's Den."

Leading the way, their hostess directed Nellie and Karl to a dining area around the corner from the room where they had eaten. Inside the cozy room, they admired pictures of beauty queens, sports heroes, and other personalities of the high school crowd. The pictures were beautifully matted and attractively arranged on the walls.

"Yes, I matted the pictures," the woman said, answering the question on Nellie's face. "I bought two copies of the school annual to get the pictures. I thought that was an inexpensive way to personalize the Den. This is for them—a hangout for the high school crowd. Guess I'm letting Pop Jenkins influence me, but the kids need a place to go, and I need their business."

"You've a nice place, too," added Karl. "I'm glad we came. Thank you for showing us around."

"I must get back up front. Do come again."

Karl ushered Nellie outside then turned her to face him. "That might be a clue, Nellie. Your name might be Greely."

"That's true, but she was talking about the city—that's Kansas City. I've not thought about Kansas City. Maybe I should look at the Kansas City newspapers, too."

"Hey, I've got an idea! Why don't we go to Kansas City? Maybe we could locate this Pop Jenkins and learn where this Mrs. Greely lived."

"But, Karl, that was twenty years ago! She said he was an old man. He's probably dead by now, though the idea is intriguing."

"It may be a foolish idea, too. But if we're really serious about learning who you are, we need to check out each hint." Karl was still holding her shoulders. He studied Nellie's face in the colors and shadows as the neon lights flashed on and off. He shook her gently. "What do you say?"

Nellie could not resist the plea in his voice. She agreed to his suggestion. "Okay, we'll go."

"When?" he asked.

"Tomorrow is my Saturday off," she said.

"Let's go!"

Chapter 7

Like two kids with free passes to the circus, Karl and Nellie set out for Kansas City the next morning. Excited and full of anticipation, they traveled the two hundred plus miles, happy and content to be with each other. They spelled silly words using the letters from the billboards; they wise-cracked and teased; they were having a lark.

Once inside the city limits, Nellie used a map to direct Karl through town to the area just south of the river. Road construction, barricades, signs, lights, and detours sent them blocks off course but did not dampen their spirits. Whole blocks of buildings were being demolished and torn out to make room for overpasses and clover leafs for the new interstate highway system.

"Never let inconvenience stand in the way of progress," quoted Karl with a grin.

Finally, they came to Washington Avenue and drove to the top of the hill. Neither had seen the Regal Theater. Driving around the block, Karl made a pass down the avenue. Nellie saw the theater first. No light bulbs were in the marquee; no show bills were out front.

"It's a vacant building!" she moaned. "The woman in the restaurant said the Forum was 'down' from the Regal Theater."

They looked for the ice cream parlor, but none seemed to exist in either direction on either side of the street.

All about them were empty lots, piles of rubble in basements where buildings had been knocked down, and a few boarded-up buildings. A pawn shop, a few used car lots, and an occasional saloon were all that was left of the Washington Avenue business district.

Karl parked the car. They began walking up the hill towards the old theater building. Soon, they were searching for some shade to get relief from the July sun. They paused in the recessed entrance to a former business.

"Look, Karl," pointed Nellie, "there's a stairway. Maybe someone lives up there. I'll go see."

She went clappity-clap up the wooden stairs. Blinking to adjust her eyes to the darkness, Nellie wished for a mask for her nose. Never had she smelled air so foul! Knocking on the first door, Nellie waited. No answer. She knocked on the second door. Still no answer. Then down the hall, she heard a door open and a witch of a woman screeched, "We-ll, what do you want?"

"I'm looking for a Mr. Jenkins," Nellie explained. "He operated an ice cream parlor near here during the Forties."

"Never heered of 'em," answered the witch, slamming the door.

Just then a rat ran from behind some boxes, dashed down the hall, and under some more trash.

Nellie, hurrying down the rickety stairs, her lungs demanding fresh air, met Karl coming up.

"You shouldn't have dashed off alone like that!" he scolded her. "No telling what might have been up there. Did you learn anything?"

"No," she answered. She was grateful to be back on the

sidewalk and took deep breaths of fresh air. "I think this trip is for nothing. I was so ..." Nellie began to cry. Her emotions released like floodgates of a dam.

"Don't give up, honey." Karl let the endearment slip as he drew her close to his side, walking her back to the car.

Inside the little Ford, Karl held her close while Nellie regained her composure. He started the engine and pulled away from the curb. "I'll drive around here to see if there's any thing that seems familiar to you," he said. He drove the car up one street and down another. He zig-zagged back and forth on either side of the avenue, but the neighborhood was strange and foreign to Nellie.

Dejected and depressed, Nellie and Karl returned to Middleton.

Nellie turned her personal searchlight on the Kansas City newspapers. Hour after hour she rolled the microfilm through the reader. One item she copied to show to Karl:

GRAVESIDE SERVICES were held at Sunset Memorial Gardens today for Allen R. Mueller, III, whose body was found alongside the railroad tracks in St. Louis on Tuesday. Young Mueller, son of industrialist Allen R. Mueller, Jr., was traveling with his mother last November when their train was hit by a troop train during a snow storm in St. Louis. She was seriously injured, but the four-year-old boy was not located. Warmer temperatures this week had sufficiently thawed the snow to reveal the child's body. Finding him brings to nineteen the number of deaths from the accident. St. Louis police searched the area for the Anderson child who is still missing.

"You might be this Anderson child!" exclaimed Karl.

"Maybe. The article doesn't say whether that child is a boy or a girl. What am I to do? Shall I call every Anderson listed in the Kansas City phone book and ask, 'Did you lose a little girl in 1944'?" she replied sarcastically.

"Hey, now. Don't be like that! You're hurt and in a hurry. Some things take time. Just don't give up hope. I'm still on your side, remember?" He pulled her to him and held her close. "Greely or Anderson or Dunkirk—it doesn't matter to me. I love you just as you are."

She knew he wanted to kiss her, and she wanted him to, but she could not permit herself to encourage him in any way. She buried her face in his shoulder, felt his neck against her cheek, and allowed his embrace to comfort her.

Chapter 8

"Nellie, Nellie!"

Roused from sleep, Nellie could hear someone calling her name. Then the knocking on her door emphasized the urgency.

"Nellie, Nellie!"

"Yes, Mrs. Murphy, what is it?"

"It's the phone, Nellie. You're wanted on the telephone!"

Jumping out of bed, Nellie grabbed her housecoat and ran down the stairs to the phone.

"Hello!"

"I've a long distance call for Nellie Dunkirk," stated the operator.

"I'm Nellie Dunkirk!"

"Your party is on the line, sir," announced the operator.

"Miss Dunkirk, I'm Jimmy Hilton," said the booming voice on the wire. "I'm with Lake Shore Resort near Mozarkia, Missouri. I'm calling concerning an employee of ours, Greta Dunkirk."

"Mama! What happened?"

"We had a fire at the lodge last night. Did you read about it in the morning newspapers?"

"No, sir, I haven't seen the papers. Is Mama all right?"

"She's in the hospital here in Mozarkia. She has some burns

and bruises. We're proud of your mama and most grateful. The fire would have been much worse if Greta had not done what she did. I want you to come—as my guest, of course—to be here with her."

"Why, thank you, Mr. Hilton. I don't have a car, though. I do have a friend who has one. Maybe he can bring me down."

"I surely hope so, my dear. Come straight to the hospital. It's right on the highway as you come into town. I'll leave word with the girl at the desk where I can be reached. Bye now."

Nellie hung up the receiver and looked at the clock in Mrs. Murphy's kitchen. It was later than she first thought. Karl was probably up. She went down the lower hall to his room and knocked on the door.

'Yes?" came his voice from within.

"Karl, it's Nellie. A Mr. Hilton just called from Mozarkia. Mama was burned in a fire at his lodge last night. She's in the hospital there. He wants me to come down. Would you be free to take me?" she asked.

"Of course, Nellie. I'll make myself free. How soon do you wish to leave?"

"As quickly as we can, I guess. I don't know how long we may need to stay, either," she added.

"I'll pack a bag and have the car out front in thirty minutes," he said.

"Thank you, Karl."

She hurried up the stairs to pack her own suitcase.

"A penny for your thoughts," said Karl, breaking the silence. They had been riding for more than an hour, and neither had said much after their initial greetings.

"Oh, I'm sorry," said Nellie, startled from her reverie. "I'm just thinking about Mama, and ..."

"Tell me about your mama," he urged.

"Well, then, do you like leibkutchens?" asked Nellie.

"I certainly do! Why?"

"I was remembering a time when Mama made some—just for me. I had an ear infection and missed a whole week of school, including the third grade Christmas party. Mama went to the store, bought all the ingredients, then made me leibkutchens. Ummmm, they were good!"

"Indeed they are!" agreed Karl.

"Another time, I remember I needed a costume for a masquerade. I wore Mama's black skirt and a white blouse that had a lot of embroidery on it. I pretended I was Heidi."

"Sounds to me as if your mama really loved you," said Karl.

"I never doubted that she did. She never said much, but she did what she could to make me happy. Oh, Karl," she said, turning to face him, "what if Mama...."

"Don't cross that bridge," he said, patting her hand. "Here's the city limits. We'll soon know just how badly burned your mama is. Where did Mr. Hilton say the hospital is?"

"He said it was right on the highway," answered Nellie. "There it is! That rock building on the left."

Karl eased the Falcon into a parking slot. Glancing at his watch, he noted, "Took almost two hours." Going around to open the door for Nellie, Karl took her hand to help her out of the car. He did not release it. Rather, he pulled her hand through his bent arm to escort her into the building. Together, they approached the receptionist's desk.

"Good morning," Nellie said to the young woman at the counter. "I'm Nellie Dunkirk."

"Good morning, Miss Dunkirk. Jimmy said you'd arrive this morning. Your mother is in ICU, down that hall," she said as she pointed to the right. "I'll let Jimmy know you are here."

The girl turned to a console at her elbow, pushed a few buttons, then spoke into a mike: "Jimmy Hilton, Jimmy Hilton, please come to the front desk." Hardly had she returned to face Nellie again when the elevator doors opened and a huge man with a big smile waddled across the hall. "There's Jimmy now," said the girl to Nellie. "Jimmy, this is Miss Dunkirk."

The big man took Nellie's hand—hers felt lost in his paw—and pumped it up and down. "Pleased to meetcha. Pleased to meetcha. So glad you could come," said the same booming voice Nellie had heard on the phone.

"This is my friend, Karl de Kort, Mr. Hilton," said Nellie, introducing the men.

"Pleased to meetcha," he said, pumping Karl's hand. "Let's move over here," he suggested . He steered them towards a lounging area off the main corridor. Karl and Nellie sat on a couch while Jimmy perched on the front of an armless straight chair.

Nellie couldn't help but smile to herself. The burly built man with the booming voice sat like a huge toad on a lily pad ready to jump. His coal black hair was cut short, military flat-top style. His speech, loud and robust, would have reverberated up and down the corridors had he not consciously held the volume down.

"Now don't be overly impressed with my size. I'm just plain Jimmy to my friends, and I want to be your friend."

Nellie smiled back at Mr. Hilton and nodded agreement.

"Good. I'm the owner of the lodge where Greta Dunkirk works. Being the owner of Lake Shore Resort is how I earn my living, just like working for me is how Greta earns hers. I have a feeling that her breads and desserts have helped to make our restaurants very popular these past few years. I do know that I'll be forever grateful for what she did last night," said Jimmy soberly.

"Just what did she do, Mr. Hilton?" asked Nellie. "What really happened? We haven't seen any papers. All we know is what you told me on the phone."

Nellie was drawn to Jimmy Hilton. His little-boy-grown-big personality was warm and sincere. He had a quality about him that she sensed went deep within. She nodded for him to continue.

"According to Lester Smith, the chef, the first sign of any trouble was when Janie Johnson screamed. He said she must have sloshed grease when she added a basket of shrimp to the deep-fat fryer. He turned around to see flames leaping nearly to the ceiling and Janie enveloped in flames. Lester supposed he went into shock, as he was just standing there with his mouth open when Greta poked a carton of baking soda in his hands. She shouted 'fire' and she made a grab for Janie. The girl had started for the door, but Greta pulled her down and began rolling with her on the floor. Janie screamed and clawed like some wild animal, scratching Greta's face and pulling loose Greta's braids. Each was seriously burned. Janie has been sent on to the Barnes Hospital in St. Louis. Greta has mostly first degree burns. Doctor Walker said she has one bad burn that goes up the side of her neck and across her eyes. He believes it was caused by her burning hair."

"What about your restaurant?" inquired Karl.

"The damage to the building is covered by insurance. Greta's quick action by giving the soda to Lester put him to work. He said he spread it over the grease pit to cut down the flames. The fire department took care of the rest. The ceiling in the kitchen is blackened, but the fire was confined to the wall behind the fryer. Pine Tree Inn, the large dining room, was full last night, so some of our patrons had been taken downstairs to the Fisherman's Cove. Most of them were seated by the windows where they could watch for the return of the Ozark Princess, our excursion boat that goes around the lake every night. Had they been sitting by the inside wall, they would have been next to the kitchen. I'll never be able to fully express my gratitude to Greta, nor repay her for what she did. She could have been crippled for life, or worse. She lost all of her hair. It will grow back, I know. I shall see to it that she has the best medical attention to care for her burns. And, Miss Nellie, your mama has a rent-free home at Lake Shore Resort as long as she wishes. I feel that is the least I can do."

Glancing at his watch, Jimmy apologized. "Oh, pardon me. It's nearly noon. We'll be needing to go to lunch soon. Here, Miss Nellie," he said, pushing himself off his chair and offering his arm to Nellie. "Allow me to show you to your mama's room. She's still asleep, I'm sure, but you may peek in on her for just a minute. I want to take you out to my place for lunch. Maybe she'll be awake by the time we come back."

The three made the walk down the corridor to the double doors marked "Intensive Care Unit." There Jimmy introduced Nellie to the nurse at the desk.

"Of course you may see Mrs. Dunkirk," she said. "She's in room three."

Jimmy and Karl stood off to one side, allowing Nellie to go alone to Greta's room. Momentarily shocked by the grotesqueness of the bandaged form in the hospital bed, Nellie just stood in the doorway and stared. Then, willing herself to walk to the side of the bed, she lifted the hand lying on the sheet and caressed the listless fingers. Obviously, Greta was in a deep sleep.

"I'll come back later," Nellie promised. Smiling to the nurse, who was busy at the intravenous set-up, Nellie hurried from the room.

As Nellie rejoined the men, Jimmy finished wiping his face with a large white handkerchief and replaced it in his pocket. "Leave your car here," he told Karl. "I want you to ride with me," he said, turning to offer Nellie his arm. "If you brought a grip, we can take it with us in my car," he added.

Chapter 9

Mozarkia, Missouri

Before they had ridden three blocks down the main street of the resort town, Nellie decided two things about Jimmy Hilton: He was a talker, and he was friendly to everyone. He drove with one hand on the red steering wheel of the white Cadillac while the other hand was constantly being lifted to greet passers-by on either side of the street. Everyone seemed to know Jimmy and the car. Even two dogs waiting at an intersection wagged their tails as if they, too, knew a friend rode inside the white car.

Nellie relaxed, leaning back against the luxurious cushions.

Jimmy smiled. "I'm glad you've decided I'm not the boogeyman carrying you off to his lair. I'm just plain Jimmy Hilton from the wrong side of the tracks. I'm one of those 'unfits in society' that the do-gooders talk about. My dad was the town drunk. Don't think he ever forgave my mama's daddy for forcing him into a marriage just to give a kid a name. There were lots of things I couldn't do. A kid like me is never allowed to forget 'his place,' you know. But, praise the LORD, not everyone is that narrow minded! Had a friend, a Baptist preacher, who kept asking me to go to church. I wouldn't do that. I wasn't fit. One day he told me he needed a janitor at a church camp. He promised me a clean bed to sleep in and three meals a day. That was better than what I was used to. I went to the camp, and I liked the work. Liked being around folks who didn't care if I was a nobody. I got to go to the preaching, too. Heard about Jesus for the first time, and I got saved. It was easy there at camp to act like a Christian.

"But the war came along. I didn't act like a Christian while I was in the army. No, sir! Then one night over in Germany, me and a buddy got separated from our unit. He was hit in the leg, couldn't walk very good. I wasn't going to leave him. We holed up in a shed we found. My buddy's leg took real bad. He suffered a lot of pain before he died. He told me not to worry. He was prepared to go. He even gave me his New Testament he had.

"Well, the Americans took the village. Then the announcement came that the war was over. I was really glad to get back to the good old USA! I got discharged. Got home to learn Mama and Dad had had their last fight. He'd broken a whiskey bottle over her head and then beat her to death. The Red Cross had not been able to locate me, as I was listed as missing in action. Dad hanged himself in his cell, too much of a coward to face trial for her murder.

"Mama had seen to it that I'd get the house she'd inherited from her grandma. That house didn't mean anything to me, so I sold it. Used the money to buy some land down here on the lake. That was the beginning of Lake Shore Resort. Told the LORD He could have half-interest in all our doings. Well, He has richly blessed. We—that's the LORD and me—first built the lodge with one restaurant. Have added cottages for the employees, the golf course and clubhouse, a marina, the stables, trails for riding and hiking, the skating rink, etc. My employees are my family. I love them—every one. Your mama can testify to that."

Jimmy swung the big car off the highway and drove under an arch labeled "Lake Shore Resort." Straight ahead was the multi-storied lodge, beautifully landscaped with a fountain, formal flower beds, and shrubbery. But Jimmy followed a curving drive that wound upward to a lookout point high above the lake.

"From here," he said, "you can see much of the resort. The buildings nearest to the highway are the lodge and the restaurants. The employee cottages are back in those trees. The marina is down there next to the lake. Beyond those trees," he pointed west, "are the stables, club house, and the golf course. Right here is a building under construction that will be a retirement home for the elderly. Each apartment will have its own porch or balcony with a view of the lake and plenty of rocking chairs."

"That sounds great!" exclaimed Karl. "Won't these folk have a view from here!"

"This will be Lake Shore Manor. As my employees—my family—retire, they can live in the manor and still be near this beautiful lake we have all learned to love."

"That's a beautiful idea, Jimmy," spoke Nellie softly.

Jimmy allowed the car to roll down the grade and back onto the circular drive. Soon he stopped under the porte cochere of the lodge.

Taking Nellie by the elbow, Jimmy ushered her into the immense building. "Here, Trisha," he said to a maid passing through the lobby. "See that Miss Nellie and her friend have rooms in my wing, please. Their things are in my car." Turning to Nellie he added, "Go freshen up. I'll have Trisha bring you to my quarters in an hour, where we'll eat a bite. Maybe your mama will be awake when we go back to town."

Nellie and Karl followed the maid up the wide stairs that divided into a mezzanine around the foyer. Across and to the right were the elevators to the upper levels.

"Jimmy's apartment is that way," Trisha indicated with a movement of her hand. "He has his own private elevator and promenade deck. These rooms are for guests. Each has a private balcony towards the lake." She opened a door for Karl, saying, "Let us know, sir, if you need anything. I'll have a valet bring up your things." At another room, she turned to Nelly. "I'll be back in one hour."

"Thank you," responded Nellie.

Magazine illustrations had shown rooms this lovely, but Nellie had never before seen such with her own eyes . Boarding house accommodations were never like this! The sea greens and sky blues of the drapes and the carpeting blended so well with the real sky and the lake through the glass that it seemed the outdoors was a part of the indoors.

Nellie opened the glass doors and stepped out on the balcony. The panorama before her was breathtakingly beautiful. Luscious evergreens lined the shores of the sapphire blue lake while other shades of green carpeted the hills. The lake itself stretched as far as she could see and then bent out of sight. It was easy to see why Jimmy Hilton said "Beautiful Lake Mozarkia." As she stood, immobile with wonder, she saw a boat dash into view around the bend, pulling someone on water skis. As it approached the near shore, Nellie saw the skier, a girl wearing a white bathing suit, lift her hand to wave at someone on the beach. What a picture!

Feeling like a fairy princess in a storybook, Nellie returned to her room. She desired a leisurely bath before dressing for the luncheon with Jimmy Hilton. Bathing in that sunny yellow and chrome bathroom would be a luxury all its own, she thought.

When she did dress, she donned a pale yellow sheath and stood before the mirror, arranging and rearranging her hair. Finally she pulled her long hair to one side, braided it in one braid, then wrapped it as a crown on top of her head as she had seen Greta do many times.

Undecided on which necklace to wear, Nellie was still at the mirror when she heard a knock on her door.

"Come in," called Nellie. She added as Trisha entered the room, "Tell me, please, which should I wear—these green beads or the white ones?"

"Wear the green beads!" was Trisha's quick reply. "They match your eyes!

"I've never worn this dress without the jacket before. How does it look? Guess I've always been a little self-conscious about this mole on my neck. But it is so warm..."

"Let it show," Trisha interrupted. "That's your mark of distinction. No one else is just like you, you know. Be proud of yourself. Hold up your head with pride." Suddenly she lowered her eyes. "I'm sorry," she murmured softly. "My mother is always telling me that, and I forgot myself."

"That's all right, Trisha," soothed Nellie. "I needed that. Your mother must be a fine person."

"She is!" Trisha's face brightened. "I know who you are now. You are Greta's girl. One of the cooks said you had come. Greta is a neighbor on Cottage Row."

"Cottage Row?" inquired Nellie.

"That's how we identify the first employee housing that Jimmy built nearly twenty years ago," she explained. "My dad and mother were one of the first couples to rent a cottage. It was very convenient for them to have housing near their work. Later, Jimmy had the apartments built. They are very nice and usually full, though the cottages rent for less. His latest employee housing project is The Village, the ranch style houses."

"Do your parents still work for Jimmy?" asked Nellie.

"Mother does. She's in charge of the laundry. Dad operated the marina until he was killed in a boating accident eleven years ago. I was only seven then, so Jimmy has been like a daddy to me ever since. He's quite a guy!"

"Yes, he is," agreed Nellie. "He has such a lovely place here. He must be a wonderful person to work for."

"He is!" agreed Trisha. "This is my third summer as a maid. I could hardly wait until I became sixteen to begin."

"Do you plan to remain a maid?" asked Nellie.

"Oh, no! I want to be a nurse! I have a scholarship for the School of Nursing in Springfield. After I pass boards and become an RN, Jimmy has promised me work at the clinic that will one day be in the Manor."

"That sounds wonderful!" encouraged Nellie.

"Jimmy is seeing to it that I have the funds that my scholarship doesn't provide. Mother's job at the laundry and my earnings as a maid do not provide enough to cover nursing school. I'm really grateful for Jimmy's help."

"He really does consider his employees as his family, doesn't he?" Nellie added thoughtfully. "Well, I'm ready. Is it time to go?"

The girls stopped at Karl's door. Trisha knocked, and Karl joined them in the corridor. Trisha led the way to Jimmy's private elevator and then took her leave.

"My, you look nice," complimented Karl. He took advantage of the private elevator to give Nellie a quick hug.

"I've two things to tell you, Jimmy," Nellie said when they

reached Jimmy's suite. "One is, I'll never be able to tell you how much I appreciate what you are doing for Greta Dunkirk and—"

"Oh, that's all right, Miss Nellie." The big man seemed embarrassed. "I am grateful to your mama—"

Nellie held up her hand as if to stop the flow of words. "That's the other thing. Greta Dunkirk is not my real mother. She found me as a little child and—"

"Hold it! Wait a minute!" interrupted Jimmy. "I'm glad you are being truthful with me. But let's have lunch. You can tell me what's on your mind while we eat. Okay?"

Jimmy opened the French doors to his private balcony to reveal a table set for three. It was laden with a variety of attractive sandwiches and a colorful assortment of salads. After they were seated, Jimmy said, "Let us pray. Father, we thank you for your many blessings, this food, and these friends. Use us to honor you this day. Amen."

Below them was the beautiful lake. As far as the eye could see were the rolling hills of the Ozarks. Seated there, feasting her eyes on the splendor before her, Nellie related to Jimmy the mundane life she had shared with Greta. "Now that I have finished college, I am determined to learn who I am. I'm so tired of being 'Greta's girl,' a nobody. I want to know my name." Her lower lip quivered.

"There, there," soothed Jimmy, patting Nellie's hand. "I think I know some of your feelings. I was a nobody, too, remember? I'll help you any way I can. That's a promise. Tell me, do you know anything at all that might be of help?"

"Not really. Greta said she was walking home from work, heard crying, and found me in the snow. That was about midnight on November 28, 1944. Karl and I have been viewing the newspapers on microfilm at the college library. About

11:30 on that date, there was a train accident during a snow-storm in St. Louis."

"Another item we found," added Karl, "was in a Kansas City newspaper. Show Jimmy your copy of that item, Nellie."

Producing her notepad, Nellie showed Jimmy the item about the Mueller child.

"Hmmmmm," mused Jimmy, stroking his chin. "A train wreck at 11:30 and a missing child may be pieces of your puzzle. But one of these is in St. Louis and the other is in Kansas City. You said you never lived in Kansas City, and Greta never said you ever lived in St. Louis after she found you."

Karl spoke up. "Look at it this way, Jimmy. Nellie says Greta sang German songs to her, so she may be German. When the war came along, it may have caught her in our country with expiring papers. She could not return home, and she may have thought the authorities were even looking for her. She wouldn't take the child to the police, but she could use the child to help herself. An officer might notice a woman traveling alone, but one with a child and without a man was common during the war."

"Could be, could be. If that's so," Jimmy offered, "she might have left St. Louis to begin her new life somewhere else. She'd save the child's life; now let the child help save hers."

"Right." agreed Karl. "When Nellie asked about St. Louis or Kansas City, she could truthfully answer that they had never lived there."

"Miss Nellie," addressed Jimmy thoughtfully, "you said that 'somewhere out there is a family who lost their little girl nearly twenty years ago.' I've been thinking. If we could get your picture in the paper, maybe a member of that family might see it. Only thing, looking for your real mama and papa doesn't make for a news story with a picture."

"I've got it!" exclaimed Karl. "Use Greta. You said your-self, Jimmy, that you'd be forever grateful for what Greta did last night. Present her with a medal, a certificate—oh, some-thing—and have Nellie in the picture."

"That's a good idea!" agreed Jimmy. "I can present Greta with a certificate of appreciation. She risked her own life to save Janie's. I'll have Bob at the Mozarkian to set it up. I'm glad you thought of that, Karl. Say, has everyone finished eating?"

"That was a delicious lunch, Jimmy. Thank you. This must be the most beautiful place in the whole state," breathed Nellie reverently.

Chapter 11

Personnel of the Mozarkia Hospital were quietly and efficient-
ly doing their tasks when Nellie, Karl, and Jimmy entered its
doors that July afternoon. A different girl was on duty at the
desk, which meant a different nurse would be in the room
with Mama, thought Nellie.

Jimmy nodded to the receptionist and led Karl to the
lounge. Alone, Nellie walked down the hall, through the
double doors of the Intensive Care Unit, and identified herself
to the woman at the ICU desk.

Forewarned by what she had seen earlier, Nellie was less
apprehensive than before. She approached the door of room
three and knocked gently.

An elderly nurse peered around the cracked door and
smiled at Nellie. Curls of white hair had slipped out from
under the nurse's cap. In one glance, Nellie saw the unruly
curls, the kindly blue eyes, and the smile. She felt like a little
girl who had been caught with one hand in the cookie jar.

"Do come in," the nurse gestured, opening the door
wider. "You must be Greta's girl. Heard you were in town.
Come on in." Like any small town, Nellie realized her arrival
in Mozarkia was known by everyone. "I'm Effie Greene," the
woman continued. "Greta hasn't been awake long. She cannot

talk, but you can hold her hand and talk to her. I'll leave you alone."

Nellie smiled her thanks as the nurse slipped out the door. She turned to the bed. Bandages were wrapped around Greta's head. Only her nose and chin were exposed. Both hands were wrapped but one had the fingers free. Nellie picked up the limp fingers in both her hands and spoke to Greta.

"Mama, it's Nellie. Can you hear me?"

She waited a moment. Again she said, "Mama, it's Nellie." She thought she felt movement of the fingers. "If you can hear me, Mama, move your fingers."

The fingers moved, ever so slightly.

Encouraged thus, Nellie still held the fingers and continued speaking. "Your nurse said I should not stay long. Just wanted you to know I am here. You rest and get stronger. Yes, I'm fine. I've finished college. I have my degree, and I'm still working at the college library. I'm still rooming at Mrs. Murphy's, too. A friend of mine, another boarder, brought me here. Jimmy called me. Yes, I'm staying tonight at the lodge. I've lots to tell you—after you are better."

Nellie felt another flutter of the fingers just as the door opened for Mrs. Greene to come in.

"Bye now, Mama. I'll be back." Nellie gave the limp fingers a gentle squeeze.

Retracing her steps up the corridor, Nellie emerged from ICU to see Jimmy and Karl talking to a middle-aged man who wore a white lab coat and had a stethoscope dangling around his neck.

"This is Dr. Vernon Walker, Miss Nellie," said Jimmy. "Doc, this is Miss Nellie Dunkirk." Turning back to Nellie, Jimmy added, "Doc says he'll take off some of Greta's bandages tomorrow just long enough for Bob to take pictures."

"I surely hope this brings you satisfactory results, Miss Dunkirk," said Dr. Walker as he eased himself out of the group.

"Thank you, sir," said Nellie, smiling her appreciation.

Jimmy turned to Karl. "I'm going over to the paper office. Want to see Bob about that certificate. Do you think you can find your way out to Lake Shore?"

"Sure can, Jimmy. You go on about your affairs. We won't get lost. And thanks for everything," said Karl.

That evening after dining on the deck in full view of the lake, Nellie and Karl strolled hand-in-hand around the resort. They wandered through some of the lanes and footpaths along the lake, exclaiming over first one vista then another. One path led to a secluded picnic area overlooking a cove. Sitting where she could watch the sun drop below a watery horizon, Nellie feasted her eyes while her ears were tuned to Karl's voice.

"According to this brochure I picked up in the lobby," Karl was saying, "Jimmy owns nearly a thousand acres of land with more than half of it under the waters of Lake Mozarkia." Turning the page of the pamphlet, he began to read:

> Lake Shore Resort, on beautiful Lake Mozarkia, provides facilities for a vacation for the whole family. You may choose water sports such as water skiing, swimming, boating, or fishing, or choose outdoor activities as tennis, hiking, horseback riding, picnicking, or sunbathing. In addition, Lake Shore Resort has a roller skating rink, an eight-lane bowling alley, and a game room where you may enjoy ping pong, shuffle board, the tv, or parlor games such as Monopoly, checkers, or chess. For the children, Lake Shore

has an indoor playground and an outdoor playground, both supervised. Lake Shore Resort has deluxe accommodations with elegant dining in a natural setting of unsurpassed beauty.

"Whew!" exclaimed Nellie, "just think of all the people Jimmy must have employed!"

"That right!" agreed Karl. "Not only the maids in the lodge, the cooks and waitresses, but those who do the laundry, operate the marina, the stables, and the game rooms. The resort has a branch bank, a branch post office, and many shops to accommodate the tourists and his employees. This place is almost like a city in itself!"

"And Jimmy knows each employee personally, as a member of his own family." Nellie related to Karl the conversation she had had earlier with Trisha. "He's some man, is all I can say."

"Yes, he is. And I'm beginning to realize that it's what he has that makes him what he is, and I am not referring to his money," said Karl.

"What do you mean then?" she queried.

"I mean God. His is not the usual 'religion.' Jimmy has a very personal, living faith in a very personal God," explained Karl.

"He seems so confident, so sure of himself, just as if his actions were being directed. Yet, he's so serene and so happy," mused Nellie.

"I know what you mean. He called me on the phone earlier this evening and asked me to come to his office to see him. We had a good visit together. He's so interested in each person he meets. He said he had two questions to ask me. The first one had to do with me, after he learned that I am a classical pianist and teach at Middleton College. He offered me a chance to become a public performer, right here at Lake Shore."

"He did! How's that, Karl?" Nellie asked.

"Jimmy says that during the winter months, the resort is the location for many meetings and conventions. Sometimes the weather prevents the entertainers from elsewhere in the United States from coming to these meetings. He offered me the chance to play 'on call' to provide the entertainment. Once they hear me play, he thought I might be offered the chance to play other places, too," Karl explained. He pulled Nellie to her feet, and together they walked back towards the lodge.

"That sounds like a good idea," Nellie said. "Are you interested? Would you like to do that?"

"I don't know. In some ways, I would. I haven't made that decision yet. But I did make one vital decision. While talking to Jimmy, I realized I needed to be more committed in my relationship with God. Seeing how Jimmy lives out his faith made me realize others need to know I am a believer by the way I live my life. So right then and there, I dedicated Karl de Kort to be a committed believer. Jimmy doesn't hesitate to let others know his stand, and I want to be that positive. Nellie, had you noticed that there are no bars or cocktail lounges in the lodge and no liquor served in the restaurants?" Karl asked

"No, I had not noticed. Why?"

"Because Jimmy attempts to maintain high Christian standards for Lake Shore Resort. He says he has families who come back, year after year, to spend their vacations here. One friend, a Chicago banker, came here when Jimmy was just getting started. He liked what he saw and has returned each year since with his family. In fact, it was this Christian banker who suggested the need for a chapel. The chaplain of the chapel is a full-time pastor for the community here at Lake Shore. Jimmy gave us a personal invitation to attend services at the chapel in the morning."

"I don't know, Karl. I've never been to church much. Oh, I went to Sunday school a few times when I was a child, but I—"

Karl interrupted, "But you will go with me, won't you? The second question Jimmy asked me was about my own relationship with God. I had to admit that I had been weak from lack of participation and commitment, but that I just realized that and had already updated my dedication. In fact, Nellie, I would like for you to know the peace that Jesus gives if you were to invite Him to be your Friend and Guide. This is an important area of our lives that we need to be in agreement."

"Oh, all right," she acquiesced. "What time should I be ready?"

"The worship service is at eleven. I'll meet you in the lobby about eight. We can have a leisurely breakfast together then walk over to the chapel. Okay? And, Nellie, there is a Bible in your room. Read the third chapter of John tonight. I want you to become a seeker. Good night," he said, leaving her at the door to her room

Chapter 13

The chapel, Nellie discovered the next morning, was even more beautiful on the inside than on the outside. The simplicity of its architecture allowed the magnificence of God the Creator to prevail. Sky, hills, and lake were blended by skylights, glass, and stone into a unified whole. A single circular window behind the pulpit permitted the eastern sun to penetrate the auditorium. The gold, green, and blue glass of the window just emphasized the small red cross in its center.

Of the four hymns sung by the congregation, Nellie recognized only one that she had ever heard before. However, she was pleased to learn that Karl had a very nice singing voice. She was content to help him hold the hymn book and to listen to his singing.

After the fourth hymn, a large man with graying hair presented a solo.

"I've seen him before," whispered Karl. "He's the pharmacist at the drug store in the lodge."

> "The LORD is my shepherd
> No want shall I know..."

The rich baritone voice was soothing to Nellie. Concentrating on the words of the song, she decided the singer had a personal knowledge of the Shepherd. With confidence he sang:

> Let goodness and mercy, my bountiful God,
> Still follow my steps till I meet Thee above..

A moment of reverent silence followed the completion of the song. Then Chaplain Davidson stepped forward. He was a tall, gangly man with bushy brown hair. He spoke in a well-modulated voice that reached every portion of the large room.

"I asked Robert to sing that song for a purpose. Many, many people say that the twenty-third Psalm is their favorite portion of scripture. The words of that song are taken from that Psalm. I agree that the message of this Psalm is very comforting, to those who are 'sheep of his pasture.' Sheep are peculiar animals. They cannot be pushed, shoved, or driven. They have to be led. As long as their leader provides something to eat, something to drink, and a place to lie down to rest, they will follow their leader—anywhere. People are like that. They, too, play 'follow the leader.'"

Nellie's mind wandered, recalling other things she had heard about sheep. Catching two questions, she turned her attention back to the speaker.

"Who am I? Why am I here?" the chaplain asked. "Turn with me to another Psalm. Psalm eight, verses three and four.. Here David asks these important questions. Their answers are in the scriptures."

Did this man think he could tell her who she was by reading in the Bible? Nellie wondered.

Chaplain Davidson read aloud: "When I consider thy heavens, the work of thy fingers, the moon and the stars, which thou hast ordained; what is man, that thou art mindful of him? and the son of man, that thou visitest him?"

"Here we have a paradox, two expressed ideas which are opposites," the chaplain explained. "The Hebrew word for man—enosh—in the first question pictures the weakness and frailty of man. Whereas, the word for man—adam—in the second question enlarges or magnifies man's relationship to the ground as the overseer of all things. God told Adam in Genesis 1, verse 26, to have dominion over everything on the earth, this ground Adam came from. Here's the paradox expressed by the Psalmist: Man is pictured as being weak, frail, and mortal on the one hand; yet, on the other hand, man possesses a dignity, a soul that's immortal, and a mind, emotion, and will—attributes similar to God. Why?"

"God created man so that man would be capable of fellowship with him. Man alone has the qualities of intellect, emotion, and volition to equip him for ruling God's creation. Man is a unique being; he is like his Creator. Who am I? A unique person. The fifth verse of Psalm 8 says that God made man a little lower than the angels. Why am I here? To have fellowship with God. Man is not like a sheep, content to eat, sleep, and play 'follow the leader.' Rather, as a person made unique in the likeness of God, man—even I, each one of us—needs to develop a closer relationship with Him, our Creator."

"If you are out of fellowship..."

Nellie permitted Chaplain Davidson to conclude his remarks without her. She was still reviewing those two questions. Who am I? I don't know. The name I have used is not my real name, she thought. I'm not Nellie Dunkirk, after all. Would knowing my real name change me? My attributes? My capabilities? My means of livelihood? Is it really necessary for me to know my true name? If I don't locate my family, will my happiness be incomplete? Karl loves me as I am. He said he did not need to know more. She felt weighted down, like a kite tugging at its string; wanting to fly but could not. I don't feel free. I want to be free!

Nellie allowed Karl to assist her out of the building after the service. She smiled when necessary and shook hands with the chaplain, but all the time she could hear the chant of her heart: "I want to be free! I want to be free!"

She was awakened from her reverie by Karl's question, "Do you know where we are to eat dinner?"

She replied, "No, I had not even thought about eating again."

"Jimmy sent me a note saying we are to meet him at The Eagle's Nest," said Karl.

"Eagle's Nest! Is that here at the resort or elsewhere?" she asked.

"Oh, it's here all right! Since the Fisherman's Cove is closed because of the fire, Jimmy opened the Eagle's Nest to the public today. It's usually just for private parties and conventions," Karl explained.

"Do you know where it is?" she asked.

"Jimmy said the elevator is in the lobby to the Cove. And I know where that is," Karl said, taking her hand. They walked from the chapel towards the entrance to the Fisherman's Cove.

Nellie called Karl's attention to the number of cars in the parking lot. "I'm glad we are walking. There's no place to park."

"It does look almost full. Jimmy's restaurants pull in a lot of business. People from miles around must come here to eat Sunday dinner. I'm glad Jimmy has reservations for us!"

Under the crossed canoe paddles and fishing net marking

the entrance to the Fisherman's Cove, Karl and Nellie entered the building. They found the elevators and rode up to the top floor, The Eagle's Nest Restaurant.

The C-shaped dining area appeared to be hanging out from the building, suspended in space. The view was truly spectacular! In reality, the dining room was well-supported by the lower floors of the building. The all-glass walls had no visible support which gave the illusion the dining room was above the earth, just hanging in space.

A waiter appeared, smiling a welcome. Karl handed him Jimmy's card. "This way, please," he said, leading them to the outside of the circle. Nellie's eyes naturally looked upward, downward, and outward. Beauty was everywhere!

Just then, Jimmy Hilton waddled over to their table. As the waiter started to hand each a menu, Jimmy waved his hand. "We don't need those, Dickie. I've already ordered for us. Thank you anyway." The youth retrieved his menu cards, smiled at Jimmy, said "Yes, sir," and strode away.

Looking about, Karl remarked to their host, "The view up here is spectacular. I can see why this is called The Eagle's Nest."

"Yes, it is," agreed Jimmy. "Maybe I should open this dining room to the public more often. It seems to be very popular today. This idea may be one of the 'good things' that comes out of the fire."

"What do you mean by that?" inquired Nellie.

"The scripture says: 'All things work together for good to them that love God' (Romans 8:28). I just pray that much good will come about because of that fire," was Jimmy's reply.

Dickie returned with an assortment of salads on a wheeled cart. He positioned the cart near Jimmy and left to return with a huge tray that he placed in the center of the table. Leaning forward, Jimmy lifted the domed cover, saying, "I hope you enjoy South Missouri vittles. Our chicken is the best outside the state of Alabama itself. Let's pray. Father, we thank thee for life, for health, for this food, for this day, and for this fellowship. Bless us in Jesus' name. Amen."

Jimmy, the congenial host, and Karl had a lively conversation, though Nellie could not recall any one thing they had discussed. She had relished the flaky biscuits and the delicious apple pie. The chicken lived up to Jimmy's boast, but the most interesting item on the menu for Nellie was the watermelon preserves. It was her first time to taste them. How good they were on hot biscuits!

She did remember the concern Jimmy expressed when he placed his big hand on hers, saying, "You are so quiet, Miss Nellie. Is something bothering you?" he asked.

"I was just thinking about that sermon. What he said made sense then, but now I am confused. I do want to know who I am! I just feel like a kite, up in the air, trying to soar, but a pull on that string is holding me down. I want to be let loose!"

"I know that feeling, Miss Nellie. Though I did have a name, my father had dragged it through the mud. I wanted to be free from that shame. When I met Jesus, that all changed. I learned I was a sinner—we all are—and I learned how much Jesus loved me. He suffered a cruel death to pay for sin, mine and yours. When I asked Him to forgive me, He did. He cleaned me up and gave me a new name."

Reaching inside his coat, Jimmy pulled out a New Testament. He showed Nellie a list of verses in the very front of it with a page number by each verse. "Miss Nellie," he said, "begin with number one. Go to that page to read that verse.

Just follow the numbers. I'll pray that the Holy Spirit will speak to you through these verses. Only He can set you free."

"Thank you, Jimmy," said Nellie softly.

At the close of the meal, Jimmy showed them around. All food for the Nest was prepared in the main kitchen below and catered up to the dining area by special elevators. One was equipped with portable steam tables, and the other was a specially built refrigerator.

"In the beginning, we called this the Bluebird Room," explained Jimmy, "as the bluebird is the state bird for Missouri. But that name sounded too uppity-up for this setting. One of the waitresses came up with the idea for this name. It sounds high yet not classy. And we do have eagles in the Ozarks."

"Diners here ought to pay extra for the view," offered Nellie.

"Oh, no, Miss Nellie!" exclaimed Jimmy. "God provides the scenery. I cannot charge for something I don't have any say about." Jimmy glanced at his watch. "I wish I had time to show you The Evergreen Room. It's the formal dining room for the convention center. But we are due to meet Bob Farmer at the hospital in less than twenty minutes."

Karl followed Jimmy's car into Mozarkia and parked his Ford next to the Cadillac. Together, the three friends entered the hospital. Bob Farmer, with a camera case slung over his shoulder, was just inside waiting for them.

Dr. Walker had removed all of Greta's bandages except the one across her eyes. Nellie held her hand as Jimmy explained, "Greta, I have here a certificate of appreciation for what you did Friday night during the fire. Bob Farmer from

The Mozarkian is here to take a picture to put in the paper. Miss Nellie will be in the picture with us. Okay?"

Nellie knew the burns on Greta's face and neck hurt. She patted her hand and tried to let her know she cared. Mr. Farmer placed her where she would have to look straight into the camera. He put Jimmy in position, used his light meter to measure the lighting, and then took two shots of the pose.

Before Effie Greene came on duty that Sunday afternoon, Dr. Walker had replaced the dressings on Greta's burns, Nellie had bade Greta "bye for now," and the green Falcon had headed back to Middleton.

Chapter 14

Their trip to Mozarkia the following weekend had to be made on Sunday afternoon. Nellie worked Saturday at the library, and on Sunday morning, Karl wanted them to go to church.

The church met in a small white building not far from the campus. To Nellie, it looked more like a one-room school, though it did have a steeple. A homemade sign out front said, "Faith Baptist Church."

Nellie was not impressed with the exterior, but the warmth and joy of the people were contagious. She was soon drawn into the service and liked the experience.

The message brought by the pastor was from John, about a woman Jesus met at a well. She remembered reading the story. Karl had told her to read chapter three, but she had become so interested in the narrative that she had read further.

Listening to his explanation of that event was instructive. But with the knowledge came those kite feelings again and that pressure she could not explain. *I must learn how I can be set free*, she thought.

Many were shaking hands with the pastor as they left after the service. When Nellie shook his hand, she said, "I need to talk with you sometime soon."

He quickly reached inside his coat to get a small card on which he had printed his name, address, and telephone number. With a warm smile, he gave Nellie the card, saying, "I am always available. Come whenever you can. So pleased to have you worship with us today."

Karl and Nellie walked back to the car. "I'm glad," he said, patting her hand. "I'll keep on praying."

After a quick lunch, they headed for Mozarkia. Greta had been moved from ICU to a private room and was able to have visitors. The white gauze bandages on her arms, chest, and hands were gone. Only the ones on her face and across her eyes remained.

"Mama," Nellie said, lifting Greta's left hand to hold between her own. "My, you look good! I told you I had a friend I wanted you to meet. He's here with me now. He's taller than I, has blond hair and gray eyes. But you can see him later. Mama, I'd like to introduce you to Karl de Kort."

Nellie felt the fingers stiffen; then they began to tremble.

"I'm happy to meet you, Mrs. Dunkirk. Nellie means a lot to me, so I was eager to meet her mother," Karl said graciously as he took Greta's right hand in his own.

"What is it, Mama?" Nellie asked. "Your fingers are trembling. Does the name Karl de Kort mean something to you?" Nellie looked questioning at Karl on the other side of the bed.

"From what Nellie told me about you," Karl said, still holding Greta's hand, "we thought you might be Gretchen de Kort. If you are, would you squeeze . . ."

"I talk," Greta interrupted in her throaty voice. "Me Gretchen de Kort."

"Wonderful!" exclaimed Nellie.

"Who you?" Greta demanded of Karl, turning to face his voice.

"I'm the son of your brother Alfred. When I was born,

Mother sent you a birth announcement, but it came back unclaimed. We've wondered for twenty-five years where you were."

"Alfred?" Greta questioned.

"He's fine. Dad and Mother are still living in the same house where you visited them when you first came to the United States. They both still teach in the same college that they did then," Karl related.

"You? What you do?" asked Greta.

"I teach piano at Middleton College and live at Mrs. Murphy's boarding house. That's where I met Nellie. This is my first year to teach. I've just returned from studying abroad, in Vienna," answered Karl.

"My papa?" asked Greta anxiously. She leaned up in bed and then fell back on the pillows.

"We do not know about Grandfather, what happened when Hitler took Austria. A beautiful plaque in his honor hangs in the foyer of the conservatory under his picture. I'll tell you this. It is a humbling experience to stand and read those words and realize you bear his name," said Karl.

"Mama," asked Nellie gently, "can you tell us your side of the story?"

"Sing opera. War come. Opera break up. Me German. No singing work for me. Find job. Cook in cafe in St. Louis. Big snowstorm. Hear baby cry. She Nellie. My snow baby. She Greta's girl. Go away. Change name."

"Oh, Mama, I'm so glad we've learned who you really are! Karl's father will be so pleased to hear from you! You have a family that wants you, Mama!" Maybe someday I'll find a family that wants me, she thought.

"I imagine," said Karl kindly, "that this is about enough excitement for one visit. Try to rest, Aunt Gretchen. Your days to run and hide are over. You have nothing to be afraid of now." Karl, bending to kiss Greta on the forehead, saw a tear escape the bandage and slide slowly down the side of her face.

She clung to his hand a moment and then released him to let him go.

"Don't run away," Nellie said happily. "We'll come back later."

It took all the self-control Nellie could muster to discipline her emotions until she was outside the building. When they reached the parking lot, they both let themselves go. Holding hands, jumping up and down, and hugging each other, she and Karl were like two wind-up toys suddenly let loose.

They were caught by Jimmy Hilton, who said, "Hold it, kids. What's going on? I haven't seen such carrying on since Mozarkia beat Lakeside at the district basketball tourney."

"Karl's found his aunt!" exclaimed Nellie.

"Greta is my father's sister!" Karl said at the same time. "Her real name is Gretchen de Kort. She is a German alien and did use Nellie to cover up her true identity!"

"Just like you said she might have," agreed Jimmy. "Well, I'll be a monkey's uncle!"

"We didn't stay very long, Jimmy; didn't want to overly excite her," Nellie rushed on to say. "We want to get to a phone to call Karl's father."

Hastily, they clambered into Karl's car and drove away, leaving Jimmy standing in the parking lot.

Jimmy watched the little green car out of sight, pondering on the news they had announced. Then entering the hospital, he nodded to the girl at the desk and waddled down the hall to Greta's room.

Inside, Jimmy carried the lone chair bedside, sat down, and took out his handkerchief to gently wipe the tears that were coursing down Greta's face and onto the pillow.

"There, feel better now?" he asked tenderly. "Your running is over, Greta. You've nothing to be afraid of. Karl and Nellie told me you are his aunt. Praise the LORD! That's wonderful! You've another family besides ours at Lake Shore. You have a brother, a sister, and a nephew who have wondered about you for a long time. No need for you to hide anymore. The war is over and has been for years. Your hospital bill is paid, you have a job waiting, and I promised Miss Nellie you had a rent-free home at Lake Shore Resort as long as you want it. Really, Greta, you have no cause to worry about a thing."

"Thank you, Jimmy," was all Greta could say.

"Dr. Walker wants you to sit up every day and start walking, too. He'll leave a patch over that one eye a little longer. He said you will be able to see fine out of the other eye. We are so grateful for what you did that night of the fire. Grateful, too, that the LORD spared you and Janie. Yes, she is improving, just slowly. She's been taken to Barnes Hospital in St. Louis."

"Good," Greta commented.

"Another thing, remember the picture we had taken when I gave you that certificate? We had Miss Nellie in it for a purpose. She wants to find her family. We hope a member of that family might see the picture in the newspaper. Wouldn't that be wonderful! I've a feeling, however, that she's going to change her name to de Kort in the future. That nephew of yours is out to get himself a wife. He certainly is a good-looking young man. Oh, that reminds me. He's playing a piano concert at the college in Middleton on August 7th. Would you like to go hear him, if Dr. Walker says you can?" asked Jimmy.

"Would like. Very much," grunted Greta.

"You do whatever Doc tells you to, get your strength back, and I'll take care of the rest. Any questions? Is there anything you want me to know or have me do for you?" asked Jimmy.

"Ja. Bring valise. Shelf in closet."

"That I will."

"Thank you, Jimmy."

"You're a good woman, Greta. I'm glad you are part of my family. Don't cry anymore. I know I fought the Germans in the war, but that is in the past. No need to fear me or any other American. You have some happy days ahead. Bye now," he said, patting her hand.

Chapter 16

Nellie and Karl stopped at the first phone booth they saw. It was on the sidewalk outside the Mozarkia Drug Store. . Karl tried and tried to call his parents, but they did not answer their phone.

"They must not be at home," he reported sadly to Nellie as he got back into the car. Just then, Jimmy Hilton drove by, motioning for them to follow him.

Karl pulled in behind the white Caddy and followed Jimmy out to Lake Shore Resort. Inside the entrance, Jimmy turned right to follow the drive by the marina into the woods behind the lodge and stopped in front of cottage four.

Nellie and Karl joined Jimmy on the small front stoop of the cottage.

"Greta lives here," Jimmy informed them. "She asked for her valise—"

"I know it!" interrupted Nellie. "She's used it for years!"

"Good," Jimmy said as he unlocked the door and stepped aside to allow Nellie to enter first. "You'll know it then. It's on the shelf in the closet, she said."

Nellie looked about the neat little cottage. In the small living room was a couch that would convert to a bed (for company), an easy chair, and a reading lamp. The kitchenette was adequate for one person. Also in the cottage were a compact bathroom and a bedroom with a large closet.

"This may seem small," Jimmy explained, "but sheets and towels can be furnished just like the hotel. It's the pictures and knick-knacks that make a place a home, you know"

"Whenever Mama was here, she was probably asleep," said Nellie. "I can understand why her living quarters would appear so barren."

Opening the doors of the bedroom closet, Nellie immediately spotted the old black valise and pointed it out to Karl. He carefully pulled it from its place on the shelf and set it at Jimmy's feet.

The valise was in a pitiful condition. Its handle was worn bare of fabric, its corners were scarred, and a hole was growing where the metal ribs and fabric met. A lady's belt was looped around its stomach and tied in a knot under the naked handle. Obviously, the valise had traveled many, many miles.

Respecting its age and condition, Jimmy lifted the valise and stated, "Let's take it to Greta. You may ride with me," he said, tucking the valise under his arm.

At the hospital, the three friends walked down the corridor to Greta's private room. At the door they paused. Because the evening shift was on duty, it was Effie Greene who answered Jimmy's knock.

"Do come in," she invited the trio. "I'll be at the nurses' station if you want me." With a friendly smile and wave of her hand, Mrs. Greene left them alone with her patient.

Nellie approached the bed, lifted the limp hand, and spoke gently to Greta. "Mama, it's Nellie again. Are you awake?" She felt a response in the fingers and continued speaking. "I'm not alone, Mama. Both Karl and Jimmy are here with me."

"Greta," Jimmy addressed her, "I have your black valise here. What do you want me to do with it?"

"I open it!" Greta stated firmly, making an effort to lean up on her elbow in the bed.

While Jimmy and Karl moved the chair in position to be used as Greta's table, Nellie placed the pillows to support Greta's back. Nellie removed the belt from around the valise, then she stood back to allow Greta to open the ancient traveling bag. Inside it were a number of bundles wrapped in newspaper and tied with twine.

Greta reached inside, picked up one bundle, and gave it to Nellie, who put it at the foot of the bed. Greta said nothing, and neither did Nellie. Silently, the two men watched as Greta handed Nellie another bundle, then another. One by one, the bundles were added to the stacks at the foot of the bed. Greta felt around in the valise to make sure she had them all, then stated, "Money. My pay. Good cook. Me German. No use banks."

"Money!" exclaimed Nellie. "Mama, you must have hundreds of dollars here!"

Jimmy nodded his head in agreement. Karl could only stare.

"Jimmy?" Greta asked. "You put? Your bank? Me afraid. Too many questions."

"Yes, Greta," answered Jimmy, "I'll be happy to open an account for you at the Lake Shore Bank."

Greta reached into the valise again to pull out a packet of papers. "Passport," she said, holding the papers out towards Jimmy's voice.

Jimmy took the papers, unfolded one, and then passed them all over to Karl. The data was there: Greta's real name, birth record, parents, occupation, and the date she arrived in the United States.

"More," Greta said as she pushed the valise towards Nellie. "For you."

Surprised, Nellie pulled the black thing closer and put one hand inside. She pulled out a lumpy parcel wrapped in newspaper and tied with twine. With shaking fingers, Nellie undid the wrapping and opened the package. "Oh, Mama!" she cried. "You've had these all the time, and I didn't know! Look, Karl." She lifted out a small, black, patent-leather shoe, a scuffed-up muff, and a child's barrette. The latter was minus the hair clip. Turning the barrette in her fingers to better see the design on top, Nellie discovered the letters "el."

Karl was standing behind her now. "Why, that's your name on that barrette!"

"So it is!" agreed Nellie. "That's how you knew my name, Mama!" Taking Greta by the hand, Nellie added, "Mama, you just don't know how many times I've yearned to have some keepsake from my real family. I had these on when you found me, didn't I? Oh, I am so happy to have these things! Thank you, Mama, for saving them for me."

Nellie removed the pillows and very tenderly helped Greta lie down again.

"You good girl, Nellie. Glad to find you," Greta said simply.

"I am, too! I do appreciate all you've done for me, Mama, really I do. I hope you don't feel hurt because I want to find my own family. Do you?"

"No, no. I happy wid brother. You need family, too."

"Thank you, Mama," Nellie said, hugging Greta.

Jimmy Hilton and Karl had been busy stuffing the parcels of money back into the old black valise. Karl put Greta's papers in his pocket, and Nellie claimed her treasures.

"We must go now, Mama, and let you rest," Nellie said, kissing her on the cheek.

Hardly had she spoken when Effie Greene returned.

Jimmy tucked the valise under his arm, nodded to the two young people, and each bade Greta good-bye.

Not a word was said until they were outside the building again.

"Whew!" Nellie said, like letting air out of a balloon.

"If that don't beat all!" agreed Jimmy.

"What a revelation!" stated Karl. "Now we've positive proof that Greta Dunkirk is really Gretchen de Kort. Just wish my dad knew we've found her."

"Didn't you telephone him?" inquired Jimmy.

"Yes, I've tried and tried, several times. But no one answers their phone," replied Karl, helping Nellie into Jimmy's car.

Jimmy carefully placed the valise in the back seat. "Old money bag," he said, "you are going to the bank!"

Chapter 17

Kansas City

Meanwhile, in a Kansas City residential area, a boy had tossed the evening newspaper onto the front porch of the house at the corner of Elm and Ravenwood Streets. This house, like many of its neighbors, sat high on a grassy terrace. Its two upstairs windows, like eyes, looked down on a quiet neighborhood. Not much traffic moved along this street, shaded by its ancient oaks, elms, and maples.

When Will and Lena Clifton had bought the stone house back in the Twenties, there had been three gas-burning street lights in each block. Later, electric lights had been installed at the corners, leaving one gas light to burn in the middle of the block. However, during World War II, it had been eliminated, also.

Back then, the milk had been delivered door-to-door by a uniformed man working from a horse-drawn vehicle. And in the summer, the two Clifton girls, barefoot like their playmates, had followed the ice wagon on its rounds, begging for chips of ice and squealing with delight whenever they stepped in an icy puddle.

Will Clifton, the head of that household, had been a school teacher with never an excess of this world's goods.

Rather frugal, he had tried to make good use of whatever he did have. He claimed he did not like to wear a hat to work. Yet that was his way of saving his only hat to have to wear to church on Sundays. He never owned a car, saying they were too dangerous. Will liked to be free to walk, bareheaded and with long strides, whenever he took the notion—which was most of the time. However, when the weather was bad, Will was ready to hurry over to the avenue one block away. He would stand in the shelter of the awning at the ice cream parlor while he waited for the street car.

But in the fall, when the evenings smelled of burning leaves, or in the spring when the flowers began to bloom, Will Clifton liked to be free to walk to and from school. He said it cleared the chalk dust from his brain.

Will did not walk much that bitter winter of 1936-1937. Ice, snow, and cold winds had compelled him to ride the streetcar, day after day. For weeks he had been another sardine packed inside the tin can as it droned up or down the avenue. At the school, teachers and pupils were compelled to re-use the air left in the building from the day before—and the days before that. Colds were many, and morale was low. Anything, even a change in the weather, would surely help to break the oppressive monotony!

Then, in the second week of February, a mass of warm air moved into the area. The predicted snow turned into rain. It rained hard, all day. When the dismissal bell rang, Will had looked out to see chunks of dirty snow and slush twisting and turning as it was pushed downhill in the Jackson Street "river." And more rain was falling!

Caught without an umbrella or a slicker, Will was forced to invade the cold wetness to reach the haven of a streetcar. Drenched and thoroughly chilled, he had shivered and shook those long blocks up the avenue. Dreading to leave the warmth and protection of the lighted car, Will's desire for dry clothing and a cup of Lena's hot tea drove him home.

Although he did not feel very well the next morning, Will was determined to teach that day. He put on his rubbers and slicker and hurried to the car stop and school.

At the end of the day, Will came home wilted and with a fever. Lena ordered him to bed, rubbed grease on his chest, and made him another cup of hot tea.

Will did not go to school the next morning. Feverish and restless, he had tossed all night. Neither he nor Lena had slept. Lena called the doctor.

Dr. Johnson's verdict was pneumonia. He recommended Will to go to the hospital. Will Clifton had never been a hospital patient. "An unnecessary expense," he said. "Lena can care for me at home." Yet, in spite of Lena's tender care, Will Clifton died March 11, 1937, at sixty-two years of age.

Lena was not left alone in the stone house. Widowed at fifty-two, she had two grown daughters still living at home. The Clifton girls, Louise, age twenty-two, and Ruth, age nineteen, were still single, though dating.

On a Sunday in September of 1938, Louise married Charles Anderson, an apprentice brick-layer employed by a building contractor, and moved out of the stone house into an apartment with Charles.

Ruth, the dark-haired younger sister, was working at one of the dime stores downtown. Her meager salary, plus what her mother received from her dad's insurance, was their income.

Although Lena's purse was nearly flat, her heart was big. She opened her arms and her home to receive her niece, Hester Wirth, age thirty-seven, in early 1941 after the death of her only sister, Clara. Since all the woman knew was to keep house and cook, it was doubtful that she could find employment. Lena could use her help.

After Hester came to live at the Clifton house, Ruth accepted John Greely's proposal of marriage. They were married the last day of June, 1941, right after John finished boot camp. Ruth went to California to live while John went to sea. He was aboard the USS Arizona at Pearl Harbor on December 7, 1941.

Married and widowed in six months, Ruth returned to Kansas City and added a gold star to the service flag now hanging in the front window. She went job hunting and found work at the ice cream parlor over on the avenue. It didn't pay much, but it was within walking distance, thus saving car fare.

Louise had already returned to the Clifton house. When Charles had finished officer's training, he had been sent to England. Now pregnant, she chose to be at home with Mama when their baby was born. Louise gave birth to twin girls on April 8, 1942, at General Hospital, Kansas City. She named her daughters Jalene Marie and Janelle Irene Anderson.

The four women and two little girls living in the stone house were often reminded "there's a war going on." They carefully counted ration stamps for meat and sugar, managed without some items, and learned to "make-do" with the things they did have. Their family happiness came from caring for the twins and watching them develop. Jalene was the active one, always moving about or doing something. She was the first to walk and the first to talk, and she was never still again. Janelle, however, was less active. She was the one to hold, to leaf through a picture book, to sing to, or to just cuddle.

In looks, each was the mirror image of the other. So much alike were they that Louise was grateful for the appearance of a wee black mole under Janelle's left ear. It was her only visible mark of identification.

The summer of 1944 was a trying time for the whole family. Since late in May, Louise had not heard from Charles. Weeks, then months, she hounded the mailbox, but no letter came. Louise lost so much weight that Lena became concerned for her daughter's health.

Then, in November, Louise received a letter from an army nurse. She explained that Charles had been wounded D-Day and left for dead near his overturned tank on the beach. A medic had discovered him alive and rushed him to a first aid station. Charles was now in the States, in a hospital in Virginia.

Charles was alive! Louise immediately made plans to go to him. She would take just Janelle since Jalene had a sore throat. She left aboard a train to St. Louis where she would take the Limited on East.

Lena tried to persuade Louise to leave the child. Traveling on a crowded train alone was hectic enough without the burden of a small child. "Charles has yet to see his daughters," she said. "One would serve for two. At least Janelle would sit in my lap."

Inside St. Louis during a snowstorm, the passenger train had pulled off on a siding to allow a troop train to pass. The weather conditions had hampered the movements. The last car of the passenger train was hit by the troop train. Cars of each were derailed, and Louise was one of eighteen persons killed that November night. Janelle was not found.

Christmas was bleak. For Little Lena's sake, as Jalene was fondly called, Ruth had strung the Christmas lights on Grandmother Lena's night blooming cereus plant and put their few packages on the floor around the huge pot.

And for Charles's morale, Ruth began writing letters to him, relating tidbits of family news, to keep him in touch with his one remaining daughter. Months later, the war ended. But the shrapnel in Charles' spine had taken its toll. Charles would never walk again. He accepted the challenge of a new vocation by going to New York to a school to learn the repair of clocks and watches. Returning to Kansas City in 1946, Charles Anderson found employment at a jewelry store on Walnut Street. Not until then did Charles Anderson ask Ruth to marry him and become Jalene's mother in name as well as practice.

Ruth (Clifton) Greely and Charles Anderson exchanged marriage vows in the front room of the stone house on Christmas Day, 1946. Lena and Hester prepared a festive dinner for the happy couple.

That afternoon, Charles took his new wife and his daughter (age 4 years 8 months) to a new house that had all the rooms on one floor and wide doorways to accommodate his wheelchair. Even their car had all manual controls since his feet and legs were useless.

Because the Anderson family made frequent visits to the Clifton house to see Grandmother Lena and Hester, Charles had a cement ramp built at the side entrance of the house. Later, he had an elevator installed where the butler's pantry once had been. At first, the elevator was a convenience, but after Lena slipped in the bathroom, the lift became a necessity.

Grandmother Lena spent days at a time in the four-poster bed in her front bedroom on the second floor. When her strength would allow it, she would have Hester help her into her wheelchair and take her downstairs. Never did she express any desire to sleep downstairs or move elsewhere. For over forty years she had been the matriarch of the Clifton house. This had been her home since the early Twenties, and she'd live here until she died, probably in the same bed of Will's death

Chapter 18

Kansas City, 1964

When the boy had tossed a newspaper onto the front porch of the Clifton house at the corner of Elm and Ravenwood Streets, it was the bony hand of Hester Wirth that had reached out the door to claim the paper.

"Close that door, Hester! You know I don't like flies in the house! Has the paper come? Well, don't just stand there, answer me!" demanded the voice.

Heedless to the ravings of the crotchety old woman in the wheelchair, Hester stood unfolding the evening paper. Leaning her narrow shoulders against the wooden door and without even looking, she reached for the hook that fastened the screen door.

"What's in the paper! Any news of importance? I wish you'd hurry once! Oh, if I had eyes that I could read." The last was not a prayer but more a condemnation.

"Aunt Lena! Don't talk like that," Hester stated. "I'm happy to read to you. Here." Hester adjusted the pillows that enclosed the gnome in the moveable chair. "Isn't that better? I'll get my reading glass. It's on the buffet in the dining room." With that, she laid the paper in her aunt's lap.

Upon returning to the front of the house, Hester pushed

the wheelchair to its accustomed place among the begonias and geraniums in the bay window of the living room. Nearing eighty, Lena Clifton's mind was sometimes alert though never as sharp as her tongue. Hester, tall and as straight as a ramrod, presented a contrast to the wrinkled creature sitting in the chair. The two women appeared more as a lady with her maid rather than an aunt and her niece.

Lena's dress was fussy with lace and ruffles. At her throat she wore an old-fashioned brooch set with dime-store stones. The combs in her wavy hair, the rings on her withered fingers, and the style of the shoes on her dainty feet indicated the superficial elegance of a bygone era.

In contrast, the white collar of Hester's housedress framed a prim face and emphasized the straightness of her nose. She wore nothing for adornment, absolute utilitarian. Even her graying hair was combed sleek, with the ends twisted into a bun at her nape. She looked as if she had stepped out of American Gothic, the famous painting by Grant Wood. Seated in the Boston rocker, Hester leaned forward and gently pulled the paper from Aunt Lena's useless fingers.

"Hester," the scolding began again, "aren't you going to read the paper to me?"

"Of course I am, Aunt Lena." Spreading the paper across her knobby knees, Hester took her reading glass and began to read in a voice reminiscent of a one-room school. First, she read the weather forecast for the Kansas City area and the headlines on the front page. Turning the page, she read the caption below a picture:

> Jimmy Hilton, owner and manager of Lake Shore Resort near Mozarkia, Missouri, is shown presenting to Greta Dunkirk a certificate of ap-

preciation and valor. Dunkirk, a pastry cook at the lodge, exemplified extreme courage when she used herself to envelope Janie Johnson, a fellow employee, in an effort to extinguish the flames engulfing her during a fire at the resort Friday night. Each woman was severely burned. Shown in her bed at the Mozarkia Hospital is Greta Dunkirk. With her are Jimmy Hilton, her employer, and Nellie Dunkirk, a girl she found as a small child and cared for as her own.

Lena Clifton sat with her chin on her chest, her eyes closed in sleep. Hester watched the rhythmic breathing a moment and then realized her aunt had not heard much of what she had read.

Hester sat and studied the picture with her reading glass, wishing newspaper pictures were clearer. The glass just made the dots bigger. She wondered if that girl "found as a small child" could be their Janelle. I must telephone Charles, she thought. He would know how to inquire. Rising quietly from the rocker, Hester went to the kitchen. She fell on her knees by a kitchen chair and prayed: "LORD, this is Hester again. Just want to thank you again for giving me this family to love. But, LORD, we are still missing one. I know you know where Janelle is. I've prayed for years now that you would continue to take care of her. Is she the young woman in this picture, LORD? I'm asking that if it would be in your will to allow Janelle to return home to us that you would cause that to happen. You know what is best, LORD."

The telephone rang.

It took her a minute, but Hester pushed against the seat

of the chair to help herself off her knees. Walking a bit stiffly, she went to answer the ringing phone.

"Yes?"

"Hester, this is Charles. Did you see the picture that was in the paper?"

"Yes, I did," replied Hester.

"Did Mom Clifton see it?" he asked.

"She went to sleep while I was reading to her. I doubt that she knows much of what I read," answered Hester.

"Good. Maybe she won't remember any of it. I was afraid she might dream up something that might not come to pass. I've a call in for this Jimmy Hilton. Don't mention that to Mom Clifton, however," said Charles.

"I won't," said Hester as she put the receiver back on its cradle.

"Who was that on the phone?" Lena called from the other room.

"Just Charles, wondering how you are, Aunt Lena," said Hester.

"I'm hungry, that's how I am. Isn't it about supper time?" she demanded.

Hester realized, greatly relieved, that Aunt Lena was not aware of anything.

Returning to the kitchen, Hester set her place at the table and assembled Aunt Lena's tray. When silverware, napkins, the bread and butter, the chilled fruit, Aunt Lena's glass of cold milk, and Hester's iced tea were in place, Hester prepared a "quickie" meal, one of Lena's favorites.

Hester pulled the cast-iron skillet out of the oven and placed it on the front burner over a low flame. She pushed a dab of bacon drippings off the spoon and into the warming skillet. She opened a small tin of hominy. Using the lid to drain off the liquid, she poured the contents into the skillet, stirring as it slowly heated. She took two eggs from the refrigerator, broke them in a small bowl, added a little milk, and then whipped them with a fork. Gently adding the beaten eggs to the bubbling hominy, she stirred the mixture until the eggs were set.

Hester divided the cooked mixture onto two plates. One plate she put on Aunt Lena's tray; the other at her place at the table. After a hasty check to see that she had everything ready, she went after her aunt, a ritual she repeated three times each day. Using two clothespins, Hester pinned a napkin across her aunt's chest for a bib. She placed her tray across the arms of the wheelchair. Then, after they had expressed "Thanks," the two women ate their supper.

Chapter 19

Hours before the sun had reached its zenith, Hester had pulled the old upright Hoover from its accustomed place under the back stairs and begun to vacuum the rugs. Aunt Lena was so familiar with the motor's hum that it, like the ticking of the mantel clock, would probably lull her back to sleep.

Hester cleaned the big living room first. This room was so large that even two nine-by-twelve rugs did not cover the floor area. A border of polished hardwood was visible on either side.

She methodically worked the cleaner back and forth in front of the fireplace with its fake "log" and around Uncle Will's chair. At one time, the house had been heated with a coal furnace and wood had been burned in the grate. After the furnace had been converted to natural gas, Uncle Will had a gas "log" installed in the fireplace.

Many evenings Will Clifton had sat in that cozy corner to read or study, or pull up the lapboard attached to the chair arm to grade papers while Aunt Lena sat in her chair on the other side and crocheted.

For years after his death, Hester had not sat in that chair, for she knew Aunt Lena would not approve. Yet, in later years, Hester had come to use the chair more often. After all, a good reading light was there, and the lapboard was so convenient for her writing. Though Hester used it now, she still thought of it as Uncle Will's chair.

Uncle Will's books were still in the bookcase beside the chair, too. Hester, unbeknown to Aunt Lena, had silently removed the test papers from the bottom shelf to make room for her own journals.

While Aunt Lena had listened to her beloved "Ma Perkins" or "Young Widow Brown" on the radio, Hester had kept a chronicle of the family. Newspaper clippings, letters, program folders, and other such items had been put in her scrapbooks. In her journals, Hester listed the daily weather, the temperature, and family activities. It was all there, a complete diary beginning when Hester came to live in Kansas City with Aunt Lena, and written in Hester's precise handwriting. When the LORD allowed Janelle to return to the family—and Hester firmly believed that would happen—she would find the family's history in Hester's journals and scrapbooks.

Hester pushed the Hoover under the library table in the bay window. The cleaner picked up the dried begonia blossoms, the geranium leaves, and other trash from Aunt Lena's plants.

One by one, Hester had removed Aunt Lena's bric-a-brac. She had left the clock on the mantel and Uncle Will's perpetual calendar on the bookcase. (One needed to know the time and the day.) But the glass candlesticks and the small figurines she had wrapped in tissue paper and placed between the folds of the tablecloths in the buffet drawer. Uncle Will's quill pen on the marble base had been carefully wrapped, too. She put it in the center drawer of his desk alongside the little porcelain box he had used to hold rubber bands for his test papers.

Putting away the "dust collectors," as Hester called them, had made her task easier. But she had purposely left a pair of vases on the mantel and the house plants. Although she did not understand it all, she dutifully filled the vases with water in the winter to provide moisture. The moisture and the plants were good for their health, so Charles had said.

Finishing the living room, Hester went to the stairs. Back and forth, lifting and pushing the sweeper, Hester made her way up the wide carpeted stairs. She was breathing hard by the time she reached the second floor. Flipping off the machine, she let it die with a whine.

Pulling herself erect, Hester looked back the way she had come. How many times in the last twenty-three years had she come up those stairs? No one knew. Yet Hester knew that the time was soon coming when she'd not be able to care for Aunt Lena nor this house. She wasn't getting any younger, and the work was becoming more and more cumbersome.

Retracing her steps, Hester unplugged the vacuum. Then, coiling the cord in big loops around her left hand and elbow, she went back up the stairs. She unwound the loops of the cord and plugged in the sweeper to an outlet in the front bedroom. Although this room was large, a rug by the bed was the only carpeting. The furniture, pictures, and even the blinds were the same as when Will Clifton had breathed his last in that big bed more than twenty-seven years ago. Aunt Lena had not wished to change one thing in the room.

Hester knew that sometime—anytime—she might come in to find Aunt Lena had "gone to be with Will." After all, Aunt Lena was seventy-nine and unable to do very much for herself.

Hester finished the rug, tidied up the dresser, and adjusted the blinds. When everything was in order, she pushed the vacuum into the hall and cleaned the runner. Unplugging the sweeper, she looped the cord over the hooks on the handle.

Hester and the sweeper rode the elevator back to the main floor. She returned the old Hoover to the closet under the back stairs.

Surely Charles will call soon, she thought. No matter. The house was clean again. Hester was ready.

Chapter 20

Frequently, Karl squeezed Nellie's hand just to remind her he was still there.

The three of them—Jimmy, Karl, and Nellie—were in Jimmy's car and were now inside the city limits of Kansas City. Jimmy had called Nellie last evening to tell her he would be by for them that morning at 9:30. They had stopped in Harrisonville for lunch, but Nellie was too excited to eat.

"Pinch me, Karl," she whispered. "I think I am dreaming all of this."

"You're not dreaming, honey," he corrected her, pulling her head onto his shoulder. "Try to relax."

"I can't! I've anticipated this so long! I can hardly believe it's true. I may soon see my real father. What if he doesn't like me? What if—"

"Sh-h-h," Karl said, putting his forefinger across her lips. "You've nothing to worry about. He's probably desired your homecoming as much as you have longed to find him."

"What shall I say? How do I act?" she asked.

"Just be yourself. Smile and—"

"Here's the parking garage," announced Jimmy from the front seat as the Cadillac entered the dark coolness of the building. An attendant pointed up, so Jimmy steered the car up the ramp to the next level and into a parking space.

Karl emerged from the back seat, stretched, then assisted Nellie out of the car.

"I think Logenfeldt's can be reached from the elevators on that side," pointed Jimmy.

"I'll check the directory," volunteered Karl. He strode across the parking area to the door. Returning, he said, "You're right, Jimmy. It's this way."

Nellie's knees felt like wet macaroni, and she had "butterflies" in her stomach. She clung to Karl for support. Karl slipped his arm around her waist and expertly guided her towards the elevators.

Leaving the elevator at ground level, Jimmy led the way into the large jewelry store. The wealth and grandeur on display did little to quell Nellie's lack of self-esteem. She dreaded so much meeting this absolute stranger that she actually shrank from the encounter. Though she desired the fulfillment of her dreams, she still feared turning the knob to open the door.

With Jimmy acting as a huge steamship, they followed in his wake through the customers in the aisles, up the stairs to the mezzanine, and to a cubicle labeled "Charles M. Anderson."

Entering, they found a jeweler sitting at his work table with springs, clock hands, clock faces, straps, watchbands, screws, fasteners, earrings, tools, and other sundry parts and pieces scattered about him. It was such a clutter to everyone else, but not to the workman himself.

Standing behind Jimmy, Nellie saw the clutter and the man sitting in the wheelchair. She watched him lift his head, deftly remove the glass from his eye, and smile a greeting to the two men standing at his desk.

Just as Jimmy reached forward to shake his hand, saying, "I'm Jimmy Hilton," the man saw Nellie. His face lit up, and light came into his eyes. He nodded to Jimmy and Karl but kept his eyes on Nellie.

"Yes, Mr. Hilton," he stated firmly. "Without a doubt you have brought me my daughter."

Just then a young man entered the cubicle, "Excuse me, Mr. Anderson, but Mrs. Peabody is downstairs. Is her cuckoo clock ready, sir? Oh, hello, Jalene," he said to Nellie.

Nellie looked at the strange young man, but she did not return his smile. She just clung tighter to Karl's hand.

"Excuse me," apologized the flustered youth, "I thought you were Mr. Anderson's daughter. You certainly look like her," he explained lamely.

"She is my daughter, Robert. This is Jalene's twin sister, Janelle. Janelle, this is Robert Bailey." Mr. Anderson introduced the men, then added, "Robert, tell Mrs. Peabody that I had to order a part from Germany. It hasn't come yet. I'll call her when her clock is ready."

Turning to the trio, Mr. Anderson continued, "See, Mr. Hilton, that's proof right there. Robert thought she was my daughter, and she is. Come." He ushered them behind his work area into his private office.

"Excuse my inability to rise, but this is my souvenir from World War II. You need not be embarrassed by it; I'm not. Here," he said, reaching for Nellie's other hand, "you need not be afraid of me. I've prayed for this day for years. Ever since your Aunt Ruth wrote me that your body had not been found by the railroad tracks in St. Louis, I have hoped that someday you would come home." Charles gently squeezed Nellie's fingers as he continued talking. "You need have no fear of me, my dear. I'm not pushy. I'll not be demanding any of your time. You have your own life to live. I know that. I'm just grateful you are alive, that you are healthy, and it looks as if you have the promise of some happiness of your own." He glanced at Karl then back to Nellie. "I've many questions to ask you, and I'm sure you've things to ask me. But instead of revealing ourselves here, let's join the rest of the family, shall we?"

Nellie nodded assent. She was too choked to speak.

Charles reached for the phone. "I'll have my wife meet us at the Clifton house for a long delayed family reunion."

"Clifton?" questioned Nellie, finding her voice.

"We are all spokes in the wheel, but Clifton is the hub that draws us all together. It's only proper that our congregating should be under the Clifton roof," explained Charles.

Like seeing a drama on a stage, Karl had watched the exchange of ideas between Nellie and Charles Anderson. He knew now that Nellie's quiet manner of speech, her almost shy appraisal of herself, and her sincere interest in others were traits she had inherited from her father. They had the same perceptive eyes and fleeting smile. To Karl, it was obvious that this man was her father. With pleasure, he anticipated meeting the rest of this family.

Charles Anderson turned to Jimmy Hilton (who had remained reverently quiet in the presence of answered prayers) and stated, "Follow me, please." Charles backed his wheelchair into a private elevator and made room for the others. "My car is below. I'll wait for you, then I'll lead the way."

Chapter 21

At the end of their journey across town, Jimmy's white Cadillac followed Charles Anderson's dark blue car down a side street. They drove into an alley between two houses set on grassy terraces overlooking a quiet residential street. In former years, the alley had been the coal truck's access to the chutes of the coal bins of the two houses. After the furnaces had been converted to natural gas, however, the alley was seldom used. After Charles came home from the war a paraplegic, he had the alley paved and a cement ramp made to the side entrance of the stone house on the corner. Now the alley and the side entrance of the Clifton house were often used.

Watching with interest, Nellie saw Charles open his car door. He removed a collapsible wheelchair, opened it, maneuvered himself into it, and with a signal led the entourage inside.

Not a person was in sight, and the house seemed absolutely quiet. Charles, as the self-appointed host, directed them into the living room. Nellie quickly made a survey of the large room. She noticed the fireplace, several house plants, and a bookcase, but nothing seemed familiar.

"The ladies must both be upstairs," explained Charles. "I thought Hester would be here to greet us. Hester is Mom Clifton's niece. She serves as her caregiver and housekeeper."

Turning to Nellie, he added, "Go on upstairs to see your grandmother. That might be less of a shock than if all of us walk in on her. My wife should be here soon. The rest of you, be seated, please."

As Nellie hesitated, Charles added, "She's in the first room on your right at the head of the stairs."

Slowly, like in a dream, Nellie climbed the wide stairs to the second floor. Nothing—the pattern in the carpet, the faded wallpaper, nor the window seat at the turn of the stairs—seemed familiar. Hesitating a moment, she wondered about the two women in the room above. Always shy about meeting strangers, Nellie clung to the polished walnut balustrade for support. She felt so alone. She wished for Karl. Her heart cried out for his strength. Then, willing herself courage for the encounter, she continued up the flight.

Crossing the hall to the first door on the right, Nellie quietly turned the knob and entered the room . Although the shades were drawn,, she was able to perceive a bulky dresser with a tall mirror, a four-poster bed, and other furniture that were just shapes in the semi-darkness. Age, oldness, and the passage of time pervaded the very atmosphere of the room.

Her attention was drawn to a tall woman who was ministering to a frail form entombed in the huge bed. As her back was to the door, the woman had not seen Nellie slip into the room and walk to the foot of the bed. As Nellie watched, the woman lifted a wisp of white hair and gently pushed it off the patient's forehead. The raspy breathing of the invalid and crooning of her attendant were the only sounds.

Just then, a girl about Nellie's age came into the room and knelt by the side of the bed. She lifted the fragile hand lying on the coverlet and pressed it to her cheek. "Grandmother," the girl spoke softly, "are you awake? Can you hear me?"

Then, sensing Nellie's presence, the girl turned her face. For a brief moment, the two girls looked at each other. Except for the way the other girl was wearing her hair, Nellie had the queer feeling she was seeing her own reflection. The other girl must have had a similar sensation. She whitened, as if she had seen a ghost. Then she exclaimed, "Janelle!"

The two girls were in each other's arms in an instant.

"It's really you! You're here!" exclaimed Jalene over and over. "I've looked for you for years! In every crowd, at every game, on every bus. My sister!"

"Sister?" echoed Nellie. "I can't believe it. I've wanted a family, but I never thought about having a sister!"

"Hmmm," said Hester, clearing her throat.

"Oh, Hester! Grandmother!" exclaimed Jalene. She pulled Nellie over to the side of the bed. "Janelle is home!"

"Janelle?" asked the raspy voice from the bedclothes. "Did you enjoy your train ride?"

Bewildered as how to reply, Nellie looked towards the woman called Hester who motioned for her to answer.

"Yes, Grandmother," Nellie replied. "I'm very happy to be here."

"Hester, Janelle is home. Do you have things ready for her?" asked the elderly hostess.

"Yes, of course, Aunt Lena," Hester answered. "I'll take care of everything. You go on back to sleep." She ushered the two girls out into the hall, closing the door behind them.

Hester gave Nellie a welcoming embrace. She put an arm around each girl's waist and said through her tears of joy, "I'm glad you girls are together again. I've prayed and prayed for this day. The LORD took care of Aunt Lena, too. I was so afraid the shock might be too much for her. She's living in the past again. She's not fully aware of the significance of this moment. Just a minute, please." Hester stepped into the bathroom to splash cold water on her face. "Now," she added, "let's go downstairs to see the rest of the family."

Chapter 22

Both Jimmy and Karl stood when Hester and the girls entered the living room. Karl looked first at one girl and then the other, recognizing their alikeness. The warmth expressed in Nellie's eyes, however, told him immediately which girl was "his."

Nellie walked to Karl's side, took his hand, and turning to her sister, said, "Jalene, I'd like for you to meet Karl de Kort, a very special friend of mine."

"While we are making introductions, Janelle," said Charles to Nellie, "this is my wife, Ruth. She came in while you were upstairs. Ruth, Hester, Jalene, this is Jimmy Hilton, the man I called on the telephone."

Jimmy bobbed his head to the ladies, saying, "Pleased to meet you."

Ruth approached Nellie and kindly spoke to her. "I'm also your Aunt Ruth. Your mother was my sister Louise."

"I've so many questions to ask that I don't know where to begin," quivered Nellie with excitement.

"Let's just begin at the beginning," offered Ruth. She waited until everyone was seated then continued. "Your mother was my only sister. We grew up in this house. Our father, your granddad, was a school teacher. His name was Will Clifton. He died in March, 1937. You've just seen my mother, your grandmother, Lena Clifton. I was nineteen when Daddy died. I had a job downtown at one of the dime stores. Louise married Charles Anderson and moved away. Then, after Aunt Clara died --she was my mother's sister--, Hester came here to live. I married John Greely in June of 1941. He was in the navy and went down with his ship at Pearl Harbor aboard the USS Arizona. During the war, Louise and I both returned home. I found work at an ice cream parlor over on the avenue."

"The Forum?" inquired Nellie.

"Yes, but how did you know that?" asked Ruth, surprised.

"A woman who has a restaurant in Middleton told me a Mrs. Greely worked for 'Pop' Jenkins at the Forum. She thought I was your daughter grown up," explained Nellie.

"The little girl she saw with me was Jalene," explained Ruth.

"Do go on," encouraged Nellie.

"Well, Louise was pregnant when she moved home. She gave birth to twin girls on April 8, 1942, and named them Jalene Marie and Janelle Irene. The twins gave the four of us plenty to do. But life was not all happiness, either. During the summer of 1944, Louise did not get any letters from Charles. All of us were concerned about him. Louise was so worried she would hardly eat, and she lost weight. In November, she learned Charles had been wounded on D-Day and that he was in a hospital in Virginia. She decided to take one of you girls to show Charles and go to him. We tried to discourage such a trip, but she was determined. Her train was caught in a blizzard in St. Louis and was involved in a wreck. She was killed, but you were never found," related Ruth.

"But I was!" interjected Nellie. "A young German woman heard crying and found me in a snow bank."

"Why didn't she just take you to the police station?" asked Charles. "Then the family could have been notified."

"That was my question, too," interrupted Karl. "We've since learned the facts of the matter. She was a German alien, in the United States during wartime. She was afraid for her own life; afraid of being caught with expired papers. She used the child for her own protection, moved to a different community, and even changed her name."

"Remember the picture in the paper?" asked Nellie. "Jimmy presented that certificate to Greta Dunkirk, but her real name is Gretchen de Kort. She's Karl's aunt, actually. His family has wondered for twenty-five years what had happened to her."

"Well, I never!" exclaimed Hester.

"Is there more to your story?" asked Charles.

So, once again, Nellie recited the drab facts of her colorless life with the young German woman who had found her, provided for her, and given her a loving home. "It wasn't until after I had finished college last spring that I actually had the time to do any research to try to locate my family. I studied the microfilm of the St. Louis newspapers and learned about the train accident on November 28, 1944, the night Greta found me. An item I found in a Kansas City paper told of finding the body of the Mueller child and that the Anderson child was still missing. Then, after the conversation with the woman in the restaurant, Karl and I came to Kansas City to try to locate the Forum and the Regal Theater. We didn't learn anything from that trip. In fact, I had almost given up hope when Jimmy called me to tell me about the fire at the lodge and Mama's efforts to save another girl's life. It was then we decided to put the picture in the paper, hoping someone would see it who knew me and would contact Jimmy."

"I've been a nobody so long," continued Nellie. "I've wanted so much to have a name, to have a family that cared for me, to be somebody, to ..."

Nellie could not hold back her tears any longer. She wept with relief, all of her tensions vanishing. Karl offered his handkerchief. Then, gaining her self-control, Nellie added, "Last week, Mama gave me some items she had saved for me." Reaching into her purse, Nellie brought out a small bundle. Unwrapping it, she exposed a pair of black patent-leather shoes, a dirty muff, and a hair barrette.

Ruth fingered the items tenderly. "I was the one who dressed you for that train ride nearly twenty years ago. Look, you can still read some of the letters on the barrette. Here's an 'el,'" she said, showing the letters to Nellie. "Louise had pet names for you girls. She called you Nellie, and Jalene was Little Lena. She even found these barrettes with Nellie and Lena on them for you to wear in your hair. We had an awful time knowing who was whom for awhile. The barrettes helped a lot.

"And I thought all along I had told Greta my name."

"You may have," agreed Ruth. "Louise worked with you girls to learn your names. You could say Nellie, but Anderson was difficult. You'd say An..., then drop your head and swallow the rest. You made it sound as if your name were Nellie Ann. The barrettes did help, though they didn't always stay in your hair. The biggest help was when a mole appeared on your neck—"

"Just below my left ear," finished Nellie. "Trisha, the maid at Lake Shore Resort said it was my mark of distinction. And you used it to know whether I was Jalene or Janelle. I have so many things to get used to. I've a new name and a new birthday. Why, I'm older than I thought. Greta found me on November 28 so we used that date for my birthday. But I was really born April 8. 1942

Hester stood up. "Excuse me, please, but I must go check on Aunt Lena. I don't leave her alone for very long."

"I'll go with you, Hester," said Ruth, joining her on the stairs.

Nellie wrapped the items again and put them back in her purse. Moving closer to her father's wheelchair, she said, "I know that losing Mother must have been an awful burden with your being wounded and in a hospital—or would you rather not talk about it?"

Charles patted her hand. "It was hard, though I did not learn about the wreck and Louise's death until after Christmas. She had not written she was coming, so I did not know to expect her. It was a real shock when the news did come. Ruth's letters were a blessing, however. She wrote such newsy letters, keeping me a part of the Clifton family. I fell in love with Ruth through her kind, unselfish letters. It was after I had taken the training for watch repairing and returned to Kansas City that I asked Ruth to marry me. We were married in this room on Christmas Day, 1946. Even then, I was still hoping and praying for this day to come, when you would be restored to our family."

When Hester and Ruth came back downstairs, Hester went to the kitchen, and Ruth joined Charles and Jimmy in the living room. The three young people were in a group, getting better acquainted.

Turning to Ruth, Charles inquired, "Honey, would you like to move to south Missouri? Jimmy tells me their jeweler has a 'for sale' sign in his store window."

"I haven't given it a thought, Charles, though I would like to get out of Kansas City. But what about Mother?"

"That's the best part," Charles said. "Jimmy is having a manor built at Lake Shore Resort. She could live there and have a beautiful view of Lake Mozarkia from her own balcony."

"She might like that. I have been wondering just how to cope with Mother, this house, and Hester. That might be the solution," said Ruth.

Hester entered the room. She carried a tray laden with glasses of lemonade.

"Ooh, that looks good!" exclaimed Nellie and Jalene in unison. The two girls looked at each other and began laughing.

"You grew up alone, and so did I," explained Nellie. "We've never had the chance to be twins. It's going to be so nice to have a sister, and a family. I have wanted one for so long."

Karl put his arm about Nellie's shoulders and hugged her for a moment. He said, "I'm glad for you. Your determination paid off. Now you know your name is Janelle Anderson."

"I'm a nobody no longer! I'm a somebody with a name, and a family. I'm so happy!"

Then Karl stood up, saying, "I've two announcements to make. I know you are all happy that Nellie has been reunited with her own family, but you may not know that I desire to make her a part of my family. Now that she knows she is an Anderson, I want her to become Mrs. Karl de Kort."

Hugs and offers of congratulations were freely expressed.

"What's your other announcement?" asked Charles.

"I would like to invite all of you to my piano concert on

Friday, August 7, at eight o'clock in Dunning Music Hall on the campus of Middleton College."

"That sounds lovely," Ruth said. "I hope we can all be present."

After they had finished their lemonade, Hester collected the empty glasses on her tray and left the room. When she returned, Hester was carrying a box. She gave the box to Nellie, saying, "Here are the journals I have kept for you. I believed God would return you to us one day. I wanted you to be able to learn about your family just as we had lived our daily lives."

"That's true, Janelle," spoke up Charles. "Hester kept the spark of faith alive in us. She prayed for you daily and encouraged us to do the same. God has answered our prayers!"

"I, I don't know what to say," stammered Nellie.

"You don't need to say anything, my dear. Just take these with you and read them at your leisure. Hopefully, you will then have a better understanding of your family," Hester said.

"Thank you, Hester," she replied.

Jimmy Hilton had sat quietly on the sidelines, soaking in all the joy of this special time. It was obvious to him that this family had experienced much sorrow through the years, but it had come through with strength and courage. He could feel God's leadership, love, and mercy through all of it. Finally, he spoke up. "I am glad for the opportunity to be present here today and to witness this joyful reunion. I just feel that we need to say 'thank you' to God, who held all the pieces of the puzzle and today has completed the picture. Would you join me in prayer? Father, we thank you for families. From the beginning of time you desired that we live in families. Thank you, Father, for bringing this family together again. We pray that each member of this family will be drawn closer to you because they realize that you are the one who arranged this reunion. Above all, Father, as honorable as the names of Clifton, Anderson, and de Kort, let us never forget that your family was paid for by the blood of your Son. So may we humbly bear the name of Christian with thanksgiving. We love you, Father. Amen"

Chapter 23

Middleton College

August, 1964

The last notes of the concerto had hardly ceased their reverberations when the young man in the black tuxedo rose from the piano bench as gracefully as a Nordic god rising from the sea. Indeed, he looked like a god, from the halo of golden hair to his slim hips robed in black. He towered above his worshippers, acknowledging their applause.

Cold chills had rippled up and down Nellie's spine as Karl's white hands had flashed across the keyboard. Never before had she been so entranced with the works of the classic masters. She joined his subjects in a standing ovation to the artist who bowed again and again.

Then, those hands that a few moments before had chorded a magnificent crescendo, were raised to silence the throng. Stepping to the microphone, Karl requested, "Please, be seated. Thank you, thank you. Now, I want to play for encore my own arrangement of an old favorite by Brahms, "*Wiegenlied.*"

Relaxing in her seat, Nellie closed her eyes. She heard the familiar melody of the lullaby waft through the concert hall. Words came to her mind—German words:

"Guten Abend, gut Nacht, mit Rosen bedacht,

mit Näglein besteckt, schlupf unter die deck'
Morgen früh, wenn Gott will, wirst du wieder Geweckt."

In her mind, she could see a young woman crooning to a little girl and saying, "schlaf' ein." She must ask Karl what that means.

Karl! Just his name was meaningful to her. She sat up straight and opened her eyes. He was so calm, so composed, so disciplined. He knew exactly what he wanted and what to do to get it.

Karl lifted his hands from the keys. For a moment there was absolute silence; then a thunder of applause. Karl stood, gave a brilliant smile to his audience, bowed ever so gracefully, and strode purposefully from the platform.

Professor Logan, head of the music department, came forward to thank them for coming. "Each of you is invited to a reception in Mr. de Kort's honor in the Starlight Room of the Student Union."

Reception? Nellie wasn't aware that such was the custom after a faculty performance. She waited until the aisle was clear. Then she cut across the front of the auditorium, went through the side door, and met Karl in the dimly lit area back stage.

Nellie rushed into his arms, returning his kiss. "You were marvelous!"

For a moment, Karl held her tight. He relaxed but held her close as he allowed his tensions to drain from him. "I love you, Nellie," he whispered in her ear.

"I love you, Karl," she replied with another kiss.

"And you will marry me, won't you?" he asked.

"Yes, Karl, but not tonight."

"Come. I'm ready to face them at the reception now. Don't get far away."

Karl skillfully led her through a side exit, skirted Dunning

Hall, and entered the Union from the back side. In another moment, he was standing next to Professor Logan and receiving the congratulations of his colleagues and friends.

"Your rendition of Bach's *Fantasia and Fugue* was superb."

"I never tire of the *Hungarian Rhapsodies.* Thank you for including one on your program

The comments and Karl's "thank you" continued, but Nellie's attention was drawn elsewhere. She watched as a large man pushed a wheelchair through the main entrance of the reception room.. Turning back to Karl, she said, "Look, there's Jimmy Hilton with Mama!"

Since Karl could not leave the line, Nellie made her way alone through the well-wishers. She reached the door in time to witness Charles Anderson wheel himself into the room. His wife and Jalene followed him.

Jimmy had pushed Greta to a corner out of the flow of the crowd. He was leaning over and tucking a pillow under her arm when Nellie approached.

"Mama! What a wonderful surprise!" exclaimed Nellie. "I'm so pleased you're able to be here. Wasn't Karl's playing magnificent?" She leaned over to kiss Greta and added, "Here come some folk I want you to meet."

Nellie turned to greet her father. "I'm so glad you were able to come. I'd like for you to meet Greta Dunkirk, the woman who has been Mama to me. And Mama, this is Charles Anderson, my real father. This is my mother's sister, my aunt, Ruth, and my father's present wife. Mama, this is my twin sister, Jalene, and my real name is Janelle Anderson." Nellie moved next to her sister and put her arm around Jalene's waist.

Charles rolled forward to speak to Greta. "I'll be forever

grateful to you for saving Janelle's life that stormy night. No doubt that the girls are twins, is there?"

"Girls alike," agreed Greta. "She been good girl. I miss her." Greta lowered her head to hide her tears.

Jimmy Hilton shook hands with Charles Anderson, spoke to Ruth and Jalene, and followed the Anderson family towards the receiving line.

Most of the people had moved past the line and were gathered about the refreshment table. One couple, Nellie noticed, was still visiting with Karl. He was holding the woman's hand. As Nellie's entourage approached, he pulled the woman into a loving embrace.

"Here she is now," Karl said, giving Nellie a "special smile."

"Nellie, and everybody, these are my parents, Alfred and Rosalie de Kort. Dad, Mother, this is Nellie Dunkirk/Janelle Anderson, your future daughter-in-law. Yes, Dad, I've asked her, and she's said 'yes.' This is Nellie's father, Charles Anderson, his wife, Ruth, Nellie's twin sister, Jalene, and our friend Jimmy Hilton. May I present Nellie's mama, Greta Dunkirk, and Dad, your sister, Gretchen de Kort."

"Gretchen!" exclaimed Alfred, rushing over to the wheelchair. "Is that really you, Gretchen?"

Greta didn't care about the tears any more. "Guten Abend, Alfred," she said. She stood up to wrap her arms around her brother's neck.

Alfred looked at the others gathered about and stated simply, "For twenty-five years I have hoped for this." Burying his face in Gretchen's shoulder, he allowed his own tears of joy to flow. Rosalie joined their embrace.

Jimmy took out his handkerchief, wiped his eyes, and

blew his nose. "Folks, you've just had a taste of heaven, a blessed reunion of loved ones."

"You didn't tell me your parents would be here tonight, Karl. Was that to be a surprise for me?" inquired Nellie.

"I couldn't tell you. I didn't know myself," he replied.

Mrs. de Kort leaned past Karl to pat Nellie on the hand. "That's right, my dear. He didn't know. It was after seven when we stopped at Mrs. Murphy's to tell him we were in town. Had to stop by as there isn't a phone at the Dunning house, you know. Mrs. Murphy told us of Karl's concert at eight o'clock. We hurried over to the house, dressed for the concert, and came right over. We were a little late, arrived during the intermission."

"Then you haven't had any supper yet, have you?" inquired Nellie.

"We planned to wait until we arrived in Middleton, hoping to eat with Karl, but…"

"I know just the place, Mother. We'll all go out to eat as soon as we're finished here." Turning to Nellie, Karl added, "You be certain that your Aunt Ruth meets the owner of The Tiger Restaurant."

Karl ushered his family and friends towards the refreshment table. It was Alfred who pushed Greta's chair now with Rosalie walking beside it, holding Gretchen's hand. Ruth and Jalene walked with Charles. Jimmy was with Karl and Nellie.

"I think this is the happiest moment in my life!" exclaimed Nellie. She reached up to take each man by the arm and pull him close.

"Even happier than our wedding day will be?" inquired Karl.

"Karl, your parents won't be able to stay in Missouri

very long. Let's get married before they have to return to Pennsylvania."

"That's very thoughtful of you, Honey. It's fine with me. Where do you want the wedding to be?"

"I'm undecided. If we're married in Kansas City at the Clifton house, my grandmother could be present. But that would appear I was turning away from Mama. I think I'd better remain 'Greta's Girl' until after my marriage and have the wedding come from her. That would mean having the wedding in Mozarkia, as that's her home."

"I agree, Miss Nellie," interrupted Jimmy. "I'll gladly offer Lake Shore Resort. As for your grandmother, we can transport her. Besides, Mr. Anderson and his wife are seriously considering moving to Mozarkia anyway. Mrs. Clifton may soon be residing in the Manor at Lake Shore."

"Wonderful! Jimmy, would you do me the honor of giving away the bride?" asked Nellie.

"I'd be delighted, Miss Nellie."

"I'll explain my feelings to my father, and it has nothing to do with his being in a wheelchair. You've been so good to Mama, and this may be the last thing I can do for her. She'll probably return East with the de Korts."

"I'm glad they got here in time for my concert," Karl said.

"Oh, I am, too," agreed Nellie.

"All the time that I was trying to call Dad to tell them about Aunt Gretchen, they were on their way here. They drove out and stopped at Niagara Falls and in Cleveland to see Mother's college roommate," explained Karl.

"I think this has been a happy ending for their long journey," added Nellie.

Epilogue

Nellie Dunkirk—nee, Janelle Anderson—and Karl de Kort were married in the chapel of Lake Shore Resort on Saturday afternoon, August 15, 1964, at 4:00 PM The bride, given in marriage by Jimmy Hilton, wore the same wedding dress worn by her mother when Louise Clifton had wed Charles Anderson in 1938. (Hester found it in the cedar chest.)

The bride's only attendant was her twin sister, Jalene Anderson. The groomsman was Richard Klingner, Karl's colleague on the music faculty at Middleton College. Wedding pictures were taken by Bob Farmer of *The Mozarkian*.

The beautiful reception, held at the lodge of Lake Shore Resort, was supplied by the bride's father, Charles Anderson, formerly of Kansas City. Greta's fellow employees made up half of the witnesses to the event.

Grandmother Dunning had willed to Karl half-interest in the Dunning place in Middleton. His mother gave them her half as a wedding gift.

When Karl carried Nellie across the threshold the next Wednesday, he said, "You're not 'Greta's girl' any longer. You are mine 'to love and cherish, in joy and in sorrow, in sickness and in health, for better or for worse, as long as we both shall live.' I love you, Janelle de Kort."

"I love you, Karl," she answered with a kiss.

PART II
Mozarkia, Missouri
1966

Chapter 1

Slowly, Hester put down the phone. Jimmy said he'd be over shortly; that he had something to ask her. She looked around the room. Everything was neat and tidy, just the way Hester wanted it, to be always ready for company. Even the morning paper was carefully folded and in its place in the magazine basket.

Her inspection over, Hester walked to the glass door to the balcony, opened it, and stepped outside. Although the sun was bright and warm, the breeze was cool. She clutched her sweater closer to her while she paused at the railing. From there, Hester often surveyed Lake Shore Resort's beauty. She marveled in the lake, the trees, the many buildings, and the flower beds, which were now beginning to show color. The whole design of the place made the streets and driveways seem as the strips of cloth used to set together a quilt. Lake Shore Resort just didn't happen, it was well planned.

Pulling the rocker to a place protected from the breeze, Hester sat to soak up some sunshine while she meditated. Opening her Bible to Psalm 23, she began to read: "The LORD is my Shepherd. I shall not want..."

"LORD," she prayed," I don't know what to do. Just nine months ago Aunt Lena and I came here. I am so thankful I got to see this beautiful place. I know it was hard on Aunt Lena to leave her home in Kansas City; to not die in the house her beloved Will had provided all their married life. When Charles bought that jewelry story in Mozarkia, she had to come here, too. The family needed to be together. It would have been foolish for us two old women to live in that big house so far away. I'm so thankful for their help. Ruth helped her mother decide what to sell and what to keep, while Charles handled the business end. I don't know what Aunt Lena and I would have done without them! I'm sure they were also looking out for me by obtaining this apartment, but I cannot afford to live here now. You know that, LORD. I miss Aunt Lena so much. She was the last one of my mother's family. I feel so alone. I am very thankful for your loving care. I know you must have something planned for me. Show me what I should do. Yes, I like this place, but without an income, I cannot stay here. Do you want me to move elsewhere? Please, LORD, be my Shepherd. Lead me."

The ringing of the door chimes interrupted Hester. She closed her Bible to go greet her visitor.

"Do come in," she said to the large man standing at the door. Jimmy Hilton's smile and the warmth of his big paw when he took Hester's bony hand showed his greeting was sincere.

"Good morning, Miss Hester," he said, trying to tone down his volume. Jimmy showed his respect to women by addressing them as Miss whether married or single. He reached for one of the chairs at the dining table, turned it around, and lowered himself onto the seat. "First, I want to commend you for the loving care you gave your departed aunt. It was a joy to see you two together."

"Aunt Lena and I both enjoyed this beautiful place. We had a nice view of the flower beds from our balcony. You really have a lovely place here, Jimmy," she added.

"Now, Miss Hester, don't give me any credit for the beauty of this place. That's all God's doing. He made the lake, the trees, and the flowers. Those majestic evergreens that circle the lake will be extra pretty when the redbud and dogwood bloom in a few weeks. But, Miss Hester, I'm just plain Jimmy Hilton from the wrong side of the tracks. You so not know about me but my dad was the town drunk. I don't think he ever forgave my mama's daddy for forcing him into a marriage just to give a kid a name. There were lots of things I could not do. A kid like me is never allowed to forget his place, y'know."

Hester nodded in agreement.

"But not everyone is that narrow minded. I had a friend, a Baptist preacher, who kept asking me to attend church. I wouldn't do that. I didn't feel fit. One day he told me he needed a janitor at a church camp. He promised me a clean bed to sleep in and three meals a day. Better than what I was used to so I went to camp. I liked the work. Liked being around folks who didn't care if I was a nobody. I got to hear the preaching, too. I heard about Jesus for the first time. I got saved! It was easy there at camp to act like a Christian.

"The war came along. I didn't always act like a Christian while I was in the army. No sir! Then, one night over in Germany, me and a buddy got separated from our unit. He was hit in the leg and could hardly walk. I wasn't going to leave him. We holed up in a shed we found. My buddy suffered a lot of pain from his leg. He told me not to worry. He was prepared to go. He even gave me his New Testament before he died.

"After the war and I was discharged, I came home to learn Mom and Dad had had their last fight. He'd broken a whiskey bottle over her head for one thing. The Red Cross had not been able to locate me as I was listed as MIA. Dad hanged himself in his cell rather than face a trial for her murder. Mama had seen to it that I'd get the place she'd inherited from her grandmother. That house didn't mean anything to me, nor that town, so I sold it. I used the money to buy some land down here on this lake.

"I told the LORD He could have half interest in all our doings. He has richly blessed. First, we built the lodge and a restaurant. Have added cottages for the employees, the marina, a golf course, the stables, trails for horseback riding and hiking, the child-care facility, and this retirement complex. God just keeps on blessing and we keep on adding: additional restaurants, the chapel, more housing for families, apartments for singles, and the convention center. The more employees there are, the larger is my family. We have such wonderful people working here!" he concluded,

"My, what a marvelous testimony!" exclaimed Hester when Jimmy finished speaking. "I'm afraid my life was drab and very common to the times. My parents owned a small farm north of the river. They managed to make a living. I was raised as an only child, and a protected one at that. I did have an older brother who died when he was five but I don't even remember him.

"We attended a small rural church but I wasn't saved until I was up in high school. I had always been a good girl, obeyed my parents, did my own schoolwork, and considered myself a good person. I did not think of myself as a sinner, so I did not need a savior.

"A woman in the church offered to pay my way if Papa and Mama would permit me to attend church camp at Oak Ridge. I did get to go, and I heard the gospel preached afresh. I realized that Jesus died for my sins, that I was a sinner, and I asked him to be my Savior. I went back two other times to help in the kitchen. I enjoyed being around other Christians and attending the preaching services.

"But that all ended when Papa got down. He'd fallen under the hay wagon years earlier and had been run over. His leg didn't heal properly. It always troubled him. When the arthritis got so painful, he just quit trying to get about. Mama waited on him and I became the housekeeper. I never went off to school or to work. I stayed home to cook, clean, and do laundry. Papa died in '39, and Mama died in '41. My prayer then was 'LORD, now what'?

"Aunt Lena was my mother's only sister. God used her to answer my prayer. She opened her heart to me when she invited me to come to Kansas City to live in her big house. Uncle Will, Aunt Lena's husband, had died a few years before the war. Both of their daughters had married, but the war had changed things. Ruth's husband was killed at Pearl Harbor, so she returned home to live with her mother. Then when Louise's husband was shipped overseas, she came home pregnant with their first child. I made the fourth woman in the household. Aunt Lena's family became my family.

"I had not taken much with me when I went to Kansas City. Selling the farm and disposing of Papa's and Mama's things was the hardest thing I ever had to do. I kept the oak bedstead and dresser that Grandpa Cook had handmade for Mama's wedding gift. That chair you're sitting on, this table and the matching buffet is the suite Grandpa made for Aunt Lena's wedding gift. I also kept the Wirth family Bible that Papa cherished. I shall always be grateful for Aunt Lena's invitation," stated Hester.

"Sounds to me," Jimmy added, "like she needed your help as much as you needed a home."

"I suppose that's true. After the twins were born, it took

both Ruth and Aunt Lena to help Louise to care for them. And then, after Louise's death...well, I was glad I was there. We all helped each other through that. But you already know of our concern for the missing twin and her safe return two years ago."

"Yes, I do," added Jimmy, "and I praise God for all the good things that came from that fire.. Miss Hester, I do have a favor to ask of you. Yesterday, Wanda Williams, who is a daytime housekeeper at the Cub House..."

"Cub House?" interrupted Hester, "What is that?"

"That's the pet name for the pre-school childcare facility. It is over on the other side of the resort near The Village where many of the employees live," explained Jimmy with a chuckle.

"But why Cub House?" asked Hester.

"One of my early employees was a woodsman named Henry Bear. He was the one who laid out the trails for horseback riders and hikers. He was a popular guide 'cause he knew all the names of the trees, birds, animals, and wild flowers in these woods. He made over all the little children and called them cubs just like he did his own Bear grandchildren. He was the one who showed me the need for a place to care for the little children while their parents were at work. Though many still call it the LS Day Care, some of us old-timers call it the Cub House."

"I like that," said Hester, "but I have never been down on that side of the resort."

"Miss Hester, there is a lot more to Lake Shore Resort than what you can see from your balcony! Miss Wanda came to me yesterday to tell me she'll be having major surgery in two weeks and may not be able to come back to work for several weeks after that. I thought of you, Miss Hester. Would you be willing to work along with Miss Wanda these next two weeks then do her job while she's home? Do you think you might be able to do that?" asked Jimmy.

"Why, I suppose I might. I really don't feel qualified for any position, but I do know how to sweep and mop. I'll surely pray about this."

"You do that," agreed Jimmy. "I'll take you over to meet Miss Lillian then. She can show you around better than I can over there." Pushing himself off the chair, Jimmy put it back under the table and added, "I've enjoyed visiting with you and learning more about you. You are a wonderful lady, Miss Hester."

"Thank you, Jimmy. I enjoyed our visit very much. Do come again," she added as she closed the door after him.

Hester sat back down on the couch, bowed her head, and prayed. "Thank you, LORD, for Jimmy Hilton and this wonderful place. Thank you for this offer of a job. Is this your doing, LORD? Is this what you have for me to do? When that woman comes back to work, what then, LORD? And another thing, LORD, I've never been around little children, remember? Just one little girl in Aunt Lena's big house doesn't make much noise. But a whole house full of girls and boys, LORD, that might be more noise and activity than I can handle. Remember, LORD, I am an old woman. Well, not as old as some, but I'll soon be sixty-five. This would be something new and different, to say the least. If this is what you want me to do, LORD, just lead me. Give me what I would need to be able to work around little children. Show me what I should do, please."

Chapter 2

Jimmy looked up from his work to say, "Come in," to the one who had knocked at his office door. Using one hand to push against his chair, he stood to greet the young woman who had entered. She had short red curls all over her head. It was the reddest hair Jimmy had ever seen. When she smiled her greeting, the freckles on her face seemed to dance around her dimples.

"Ah, yes," smiled Jimmy, "I remember now. You are Lydia Carson's lovely daughter. Sarah, what can I do for you?"

Sarah was surprised but delighted that Jimmy remembered her name.. She was quick to sober, however, and said, "I know you have other things to do, so I will be brief. I learned at work last evening that Wanda Williams will need surgery. I would like to ask to take her place. The extra money would certainly come in handy right now."

"Sit down, Sarah," Jimmy said. "Now talk to me. I thought you were taking classes at the local college. How would you be able to work the day shift at the Cub House? Why this sudden desire for additional wages?"

"Yes, sir, I am, but a situation has come up in the family. Mother and I have agreed that I might lay out this term and get a better-paying job in order to contribute towards this need. Hopefully I could resume college next term."

"And this need?" Jimmy inquired.

"I'd rather not say," Sarah replied politely. "You will consider me, won't you, Jimmy?" she asked, rising from her chair.

"Yes, Sarah, I'll give your need careful thought. Thank you for coming by."

After she left, Jimmy looked up a number and dialed the phone. "Miss Lydia, this is Jimmy. I need to talk to you. May I come over?"

"Of course, Jimmy. I rather expected you to call."

"I'll be right over. Thank you."

Jimmy left his office on the mezzanine of the lodge, entered his private elevator, and exited in the garage where his big white Cadillac was housed. In years past, Jimmy had walked everywhere and anywhere on the resort. But since he'd become older and heavier, he now drove about the resort. This trip was to The Village, where many of his employees had homes.

He rang the bell and was immediately invited inside the Carson home. Lydia was a widow who had lived at Lake Shore Resort for many years. Robert Carson, her husband, had drowned attempting to save a child who had fallen off the deck of the excursion boat. Jimmy had granted Lydia a home on the resort for as long as she needed it. Sarah had been quite small then. Lydia had done well to teach her the value of work in order to have the extras that life has to offer.

"Good morning, Jimmy," Lydia greeted her visitor. "I just knew you would come as soon as you heard. Sarah and I decided last night what we could do to help. She would ask you for longer hours."

"She did that, Miss Lydia. I need to know why. How can I help if I do not know the problem?"

"Jimmy, it's not for me directly, but for my sister Martha.

She lives with her daughter in Lakeville. Roseann was coming home from a school activity a few weeks ago and was hit by a drunken driver. He ran a red light and plowed his pickup into the side of Roseann's car. He wasn't hurt, but she has a broken leg and a demolished car. She's on crutches now, trying to finish her senior year in high school. It's been quite a hardship on them, this not having a car. Martha is having to depend on friends and neighbors to take her to the store and other errands. After awhile that gets old. She hates being a pest. I live too far away to be much help. So Sarah and I decided we could send Martha some cash to help her pay her bills and postage."

"Does she not have any other family?" asked Jimmy.

"No, our parents have been gone a long time. And her husband's parents died when he was a boy. In fact, William was raised by an aunt who is also gone. He never had a real family. That may have been why he worked so hard to provide a loving one for his own children." Lydia added.

"Did you say children?" interrupted Jimmy.

"Yes, William and Martha have a son, Richard, and their daughter is Roseann. Richard's a fine young man, none better. But he was not able to handle being around home after his dad was killed by a drunken driver, no less. That's another thing that has made this so hard on Martha. Roseann's accident has just refreshed the memories about William's death. She's had to relive the pain and loss all over again. We're just thankful Roseann was not killed in this crash."

"Miss Lydia," Jimmy inquired, "do you have a recent picture of your nephew?"

"Yes, of course. I have his senior picture when he graduated three years ago. I'll go get it."

While Lydia went to get the picture, Jimmy pondered

how he might search for and learn where this young man was living.

Lydia handed the small photo to Jimmy, saying, "I took it out of the folder to make it easier to carry."

Jimmy studied the photo a minute. "Tell me, Miss Lydia, what does Richard like to do? What skills does he have? Is he a musician, a carpenter, or a mechanic? Just what kind of work might he be doing?"

Laughing, Lydia replied, "A musician he definitely is not! He 'played' with his Tinker Toys when he was a little boy. He used to hang around his dad's garage a lot when he got older. William was a mechanic and always had someone's car in his shop. I don't know about Richard, if he's like his dad or not. Afraid I can't be much help there."

"Another question," said Jimmy, reaching into the inside pocket of his suit coat for a writing pad. "I need to know some family names, if you please. I know you are Lydia Carson and your husband was Robert. Who were his folks?"

"I don't know that, and neither did Robert. He was adopted as a baby and raised by Kenneth and Vera Carson. Martha and I are the only ones left of our kin. Our parents were George and Naomi Underwood. But why the names?"

"That young man is hiding. He may be using another name within the family. Just might be helpful for me to know. He needs to know that he is needed at home. I'll see if we can find him. Meanwhile, I'll see what I can do to be of assistance. I just hope Sarah does not need to drop out of college. Thank you, Miss Lydia, for this information."

"Thank you, Jimmy," Lydia said as she bade him good-bye.

Jimmy drove the white Caddy out the main entrance of the

resort and down the highway to Mozarkia. He went straight to the police station to have a visit with Bob Summers.

Bob was on the phone. He waved Jimmy to a seat and soon ended his conversation. He strode towards Jimmy with an outstretched hand. As they shook hands, he inquired, "Good to see you, buddy. What can I do for you?" He sat on the corner of his desk, waiting.

Jimmy took the photo from his inside pocket and gave it to Bob. "Have you ever seen this young man?" he asked.

Bob looked at the picture. He laid his forefinger over the lower portion of the face. He covered the hairline with his finger, continuing to study the face. "I may have, just don't know for sure. He may have had a cap on, or a mustache, but there is something about that face that does look familiar. Why, what has he done?"

"I don't know that he has done anything. His dad was killed in an accident with a drunken driver. The boy's grief drove him away from home. There has been another drunken-driver related accident in the family. This time his sister's car was hit, and she has a broken leg. I want to find him. He is needed at home!"

"Okay. Give me some dope."

"His name is Richard Nelson. Family's address is Lakeville. He graduated from high school three years ago. He would be about 21 years of age now. His parents were William and Martha Nelson. His sister's name is Roseann. She is a senior in high school this year. His aunt is Lydia Underwood Carson who lives at Lake Shore Resort."

"Well, Jimmy, the first thing I can do is check with social security to see if there has been any activity there. If he is employed and using another name, there won't be. In that case, we're in for a longer search," added Bob.

Jimmy gave Bob the page from his memo pad. "Here are some other family names just in case you need them. Whatever you do, please do not post his mug in the post office as some common criminal. He's disturbed and left home to try to forget."

"I'll be very discreet. Trust me, Jimmy."

Jimmy shook his hand saying, "Thanks, Bob," and left the police station.

Chapter 3

Hester lifted the telephone. Immediately the girl at the switchboard inquired, "How may I help you?"

"May I speak with Jimmy Hilton, please?"

"One moment, please." After a pause she said, "I'm sorry. Jimmy is away from his office just now. May I take a message?"

"Please tell him Hester Wirth called. Thank you."

Hester hung up the phone. She picked up her shawl and went out on the balcony. Tossing the shawl about her shoulders, she sat in the rocker and picked up her Bible. She opened it to the book of Exodus. Turning to chapter four, she began to read the conversation God had with Moses at the burning bush.

"And the LORD said to him, 'What is that in your hand?' And he said, 'A staff'" (Exodus 4:2).

Hester paused in her reading. "LORD," she prayed, "you called Moses to lead all those people out of Egypt so many years ago. He was just a shepherd. All he had in his hand was a shepherd's crook. Yet you used it to have him perform such marvelous deeds. LORD, you know me. You know what I can do with my hands. Use what I have to honor—"

The door chimes aroused Hester. She went to answer the door.

"Come in, Jimmy," Hester invited.

"I got your message, Miss Hester. Hope you have made a decision about my offer," he said . He pulled the dining chair out from the table and turned it for him to sit.

"Yes, I have, but it may not be the answer you expect. I just do not feel that I should try to do that job. I have the feeling that there is something else here God wants me to do, something more like me. Being around little children is foreign to me. I just feel a strangeness, like God is saying to wait; that what he wants for me will show up later. I feel that I need to trust him and wait. I am so sorry if I've left you with a vacancy—"

"No, no, Miss Hester," interrupted Jimmy. "Through you, God has answered my prayer as well as yours. You see, the very next morning after I was here, I had a lady come asking for that job. She has a particular need right now and hoped the pay would cover those expenses. That put me in the middle, you see. I wanted to help her, but I'd already offered the position to you. Your rejection frees me to let her have it. See how the LORD works things out! We both trusted him to do what was best for everyone."

"Thank you, Jimmy, for coming. I do feel better knowing you do have someone to help Mrs. Williams," she said as she closed the door behind him.

The smartly dressed young woman alighted from the bus, accepted her suitcase from the driver, and stepped up on the sidewalk. She stood out of the way while three other passengers collected their luggage and went into the station. The driver checked his list, slammed shut the cargo door, and followed the others inside.

Jalene Anderson looked up and down the street, but no cab was in sight. Just then a young man came out of the drug store next door. He smiled at the lovely young woman in the navy suit. Noticing her suitcase, he asked, "Need directions?"

"Not exactly. I know where I'm going, I just don't see a cab to get me there," she replied.

"Maybe I can help. I'm not a native, but I do know my way around in these parts."

"Lake Shore?" she queried.

"Sure! Let me get the keys and I'll drive you there myself." He returned to the drug store, opened the door, and called to his friend, "Buddy, toss me your keys. Need to take this lady out to LS." He caught the keys and returned to take the suitcase from Jalene. He put it in the back seat of a car at the curb, opened the front door for her, and then dashed around to get under the wheel.

"My name is Richard," he said. "This happens to be my day off, or I would be assembling engines for boats like you can see out on the lake yonder." He pointed towards the water beyond the trees.

Jalene had already noticed the sparkling water of the lake. "I'm Jalene Anderson. I'm on spring break. No, I'm not a college student, but I do work in an office on campus. I chose to take some time off while the students were having a vacation. My parents just recently moved to Mozarkia, but I still live in Kansas City."

"Do your parents live at Lake Shore?" he asked.

"No, they live in town. They are having some work done on the house to accommodate my dad. He is confined to a wheelchair due to a spinal injury in the war. They do not have a place for me just now."

"Am I to take you to the lodge, then?" Richard asked.

"No, I need to go the apartment complex that's up on the hill above the lodge. It may have a name, I just don't know it. That's where Hester lives. She's my grandmother's niece. Really, she is more than that. Hester was my grandmother's nurse, housekeeper, and companion for over twenty years. What about you, Richard? You said you were not a native. Where are you from?"

"Oh, I'm from a wide place in the road up north a ways. I came here to work. I didn't want to be a burden on my mom after Dad died."

"It's hard to lose a parent, I know. My mother was killed in a train accident. I was only two, so I don't remember her at all."

"Well, I'm not quite like that. I had my dad growing up. He was killed in an auto crash the summer after I finished high school. A drunk hit him head-on. I do have a lot of good memories, but I still miss him. I have so many things I'd like to ask him."

"I can empathize with that somewhat. I lost my twin sister in the accident that killed my mother. I grew up as the only child in a big house with three women. How many times I wished for my sister! God gave her back to us two years ago. We've talked and talked, but it's not the same. Both of us had experienced loneliness and years of being alone. You mentioned your mother. Do you have any siblings?"

"Yes, I have one sister," said Richard. "She's a senior in high school."

"That's wonderful!" Jalene interjected.

Richard pulled the car into the parking lot at the Lake Shore Manor and parked next to a white Cadillac. He turned off the engine and turned towards Jalene. "Thank you for such an enjoyable conversation. You are certainly easy to talk with. I have hardly talked with a girl since leaving home."

"I enjoyed it, too, Richard. Would you let me pay you this for taxi fare?" she asked as she held out some bills.

"No, no, the pleasure was all mine. Here, allow me to carry your suitcase inside," he added as he assisted Jalene from the car.

Just then Jimmy Hilton came around the corner of the building, heading for his Caddy. He saw the two young people and recognized Jalene Anderson.

"Hello, good to see you again," Jimmy boomed as he approached the couple.

"Why, Jimmy Hilton! What a pleasant surprise! I came to visit Hester. Do hope she is well?"

"She's fine, fine."

Richard put down the suitcase, got back in the car, and started the motor. Jalene dashed over to the car, saying, "Thank you again, Richard, for bringing me out. Maybe we'll see each other again."

"I'd like that," he said. "Bye."

Jimmy had moved to where he could see the upturned face of the young man as he ended his conversation with Jalene. He turned to her and asked, "Who was that young fellow? He sure seemed to be in a hurry to leave."

"His name is Richard. Now that I think about it, he didn't say what his last name was."

Jimmy took the picture from his inside suit pocket. "Does this look like him to you?"

"Yes, Jimmy. That's Richard, no doubt about it. But why do you have his picture?" she asked.

"Because I am trying to find him. He is needed at home," said Jimmy.

"Maybe I can help. He has a job in town assembling boat motors. Today was his day off. The car he drove belongs to a friend who was in the drug store next to the bus station. He called him Buddy."

"Did he mention his family?"

"Yes, he told me of his father's death and that his sister is a senior this year. He said he came here to work to make it easier on his mother."

"Well, they do not know where he is, or even if he's still alive. They haven't heard from him in nearly three years. There's been another accident, and his sister is on crutches. His mother needs him. Thanks for the information. Enjoy your visit with Hester and your folks."

Jimmy got in his car and headed for Mozarkia, hoping to catch Richard.

Meanwhile, Jalene picked up her suitcase, went inside the apartment house, and rode the elevator up to Hester's floor.

Chapter 4

Jimmy found a parking space, emerged from his car, and was nearly to the drug store when Richard exited the building.

"Richard?" called Jimmy. The young man turned to see who had called his name.

"Your name is Richard, isn't it?" Jimmy inquired as he offered his beefy hand.

"Yes, but how come you to know that?" he asked hesitatingly.

"Aw, don't be afraid of me, son. I'm just plain ole Jimmy, and I want to visit with you a few minutes. Let's go over here to sit down." Jimmy led the way to the empty bench in front of the bus station. Passersby spoke to Jimmy or waved. He returned the greetings but continued talking.

Richard was intrigued by the huge man whose voice was like a rumble of thunder. Yet he was so calming and gentle that it seemed to touch and soothe.

Jimmy reached inside his coat for the picture. Showing it to Richard, he explained, "Your Aunt Lydia is part of my family, Richard. She lives at Lake Shore, y'know. We all work together and help each other. Your family has been worrying about you for a long time now." He reached over to pat Richard on the knee. "Your sister's car was hit by a drunken driver and—"

"She's all right, isn't she?" interrupted Richard.

"She's doing quite well. Her leg was broken, so she is back in school on crutches. But the car was demolished. That has put an extra burden on your mama. Now she has to ask a friend or a neighbor to drive her on errands—"

"And this has reminded her of Dad's accident all over again. Poor Mama!" He dropped his head in his hands.

"Richard," Jimmy said softly, "your mama needs you, and your sister needs you. You are needed at home. They don't even know if you are alive or dead."

"I've wanted to write, even started a letter a few times. I just didn't know what to say. I decided it was easier on Mama to have one less mouth to feed. Tell me, Jimmy, how did you get a picture of me? Who told you all of this?"

"Your Aunt Lydia. Sarah came to me to ask for a full-time job. She and her mother had decided for her to lay out of college one term. She'd work full-time on the day shift. The extra funds would go to help Martha and Roseann to pay their bills."

"She shouldn't have to do that! We are related, I know, but my family should not be their responsibility!" he said. "I see it now. With Dad gone, I am the one who should be helping Mama, not her sister. Instead, I ran away. That was not being mature, was it? I acted like a kid."

"Now don't be too hard on yourself. You were young then. The events and your grief just overwhelmed you at the time. Looks to me like you have learned some things about life. Don't imagine it was easy being out on your own like that. I know it wasn't for me. When I came home from the war, I found my dad in jail for killing my mama. He was drunk. Instead of facing a trial, he hanged himself. Mama had left me a bit of property. I sold it to buy land down here on the lake. I just wanted to be alone. When I came to my senses, I asked God to be my partner in this enterprise. He has surely blessed. This resort is a means to help others. I don't know how I could have done what I did if God had not been with me in it. Richard, we need to decide how we can help your family," stated Jimmy.

"Sounds like Mama needs a car, for one thing. I've been saving some, but I don't have enough for even a down payment yet," Richard replied.

"Could we make a deal, Richard? I'll help you buy one. You can pay me instead of a bank, and I don't charge interest on my loans," Jimmy added.

"Wow! That sounds like a good deal!" exclaimed Richard.

"I want you to go home, to spend some time with your family, and— "

"But what about my job?" interrupted Richard.

"Where are you working?" inquired Jimmy.

"I'm an assemblyman at SeaSpray Motors," he answered.

"You will need to give your employer at least two weeks notice. Just don't quit. Never do that. Giving him notice will help establish your credibility. Only then can you expect an employer to give you a job reference. Do you enjoy working on motors?" asked Jimmy.

"Yes, I do! Dad was a mechanic. He worked on cars. I learned a lot by helping him. I prefer smaller engines myself, like those on boats, chain saws, and such," he answered.

"That's great!" exclaimed Jimmy. "Tell you what. It seems like there are always more to be fixed than there are men to do the fixing at the marina at Lake Shore. I will have a job for you in the maintenance garage when you return to Mozarkia. How does that sound?"

"That sounds great! I don't know how to thank you!"

Rising from the bench, Jimmy put out his hand again. "Glad to meet you, Richard," he said, shaking his hand. "You go shop for that sensible vehicle your family needs, then let me know when you find it. Give your boss notice of your leaving. And it won't hurt anything if you tell him why. Pay all your debts. Your dad left you with a good name, so do nothing to smear it. Take all your stuff with you when you go home. And Richard, God is the one who brought us together. You might want to thank him for that."

"Thanks, Jimmy. I'll do that. See you soon."

Jimmy returned to his car and breathed his own prayer of thanks. He turned the key and drove to the police station.

Chapter 5

Hester had just laid her shawl on her bed when the door chimes sounded. Jimmy must have forgotten something, she thought as she went back to the door.

"Jalene! What a surprise!" was all she got to say before the two were in a close embrace.

"Oh, Hester! It's so good to see you!"

Hester pushed the door closed with one hand. With the other hand she pulled Jalene over to the couch. "Now, tell me. Why are you here on a work day? Are you ill?"

"Oh, no, Hester, I'm fine! This is spring break. Colleges have a week off before they begin the final term. I chose to use some of my vacation time to get out of Kansas City for a few days. Since Dad and Mom's house is being redone, I came here. I hope you'll let me use your spare bedroom. May I?" Jalene questioned.

"Of course, of course you may. How did you get here, honey? Did you drive?" Hester asked.

"No, I came on the bus to Mozarkia. Got a ride out here. I need to call the folks to let them know I am here. I had not told them I was coming," she added.

"Yes, do that," agreed Hester as she headed towards the kitchen.

A few minutes later, Hester led the way to her favorite

place on the balcony. Jalene followed, carrying the tray laden with a tea service and a plate of fresh-baked banana bread. Jalene put the tray on the low table by Hester's rocker. She went to stand at the railing to admire the view.

"This must be one of God's most beautiful places! Just look at the tall evergreens, the lake, the sky—it's really lovely. From here the resort looks like one huge quilt, each piece in place by design." said Jalene as she breathed in the fresh air.

"Jimmy gives God credit for the beauty and the master design," Hester said as she poured the tea. After each had tea to drink and bread to nibble, Hester said, "Now, tell me what you have been doing."

"Oh, I sleep nights and work days. I'm just thankful my apartment is close to my work, which allows me to walk to and from. But what about you, Hester? What do you do to keep busy? I know you must really miss Grandmother Lena," said Jalene.

"I do, yes, I do. I know she's safe in the arms of Jesus. I am trusting the LORD to continue to care for me. I'll share this with you. Jimmy Hilton came the other morning to see if I'd like to fill in for a lady who's to have surgery in a few weeks. That made me feel good 'cause I do need something to do, but the work was to do housekeeping at the Cub House. That is the pre-school childcare facility here at the resort. I could do the housekeeping. But Jalene, I've never been around little children. You know that. Just you in that big house in Kansas City is one thing. But a whole roomful of boys and girls would be something else. I just didn't know about that."

"What did you tell Jimmy?" asked Jalene.

"I said I would have to pray about the matter, which I did. The LORD did not give me peace. He seemed to be saying for me to wait. I called Jimmy. He wasn't there, but he did come see me."

"And?"

"This is the good part. I really hated to tell him I couldn't accept his offer. I knew he really needed someone. But the day after he asked me, another person came to him, asking for the job. She was someone who really needed to work full-time. My declining freed him to allow this person to have the job. Isn't that the way God cares for us?"

"Yes, it is, Hester," agreed Jalene, "but now what?"

"That's exactly what I asked the LORD! I'm nearly sixty-five years old. I've never worked, never earned a dollar, never paid Social Security, never filed an income tax—I was always someone's dependant—and I never learned to drive a car. The list of what I can't do goes on and on."

"That may be true, Hester, but you can cook, clean, and care for others."

"I just pray the LORD will continue to provide for me. I don't know what else to do."

Jalene took Hester's hands in hers and talked woman to woman. "Hester, I know you are frustrated. So am I. I'm stuck in Kansas City, away from the family. My friends are all married and have families. I feel like I'm all thumbs and no fingers when I am with any of them. My days are so routine: go to work, go home, go to church, go home, day after day after day. I am ready for a change. Here's a suggestion that might benefit both of us. We shall have to pray to see if this is what God has in mind for us," said Jalene.

"What is your suggestion, Jalene?" asked Hester.

"I have one more term at the college on my present contract. I'll give notice that I will not be renewing. My services, therefore, will end May 31st. I can move down here. I can talk to Jimmy to see if I could live here in this apartment with you. I could pay the rent, and you can do what you do best: Cook, clean, and care for someone—me."

"That sounds wonderful for me. But where would you work?" asked Hester.

"I am really not concerned about that. There'll be some business that needs a bookkeeper or an accountant. I can always hang out my shingle as a CPA or do income tax returns. Who knows, Jimmy might need a CPA on his staff here at the resort. We'll pray about this. If it is God's will, He will work out all those details and answer the big questions," replied Jalene.

Just then the telephone rang. "I'll get it. That may be Mother calling to check on you. No one answered when I called earlier."

Jalene went inside to answer the phone. She returned to the doorway to ask, "Hester, are you up to going out to dinner? Dad and Mom want to come for us about 6:30 if you are agreeable."

"That will be fine," Hester replied. "Oh, thank you, LORD. Thank you, thank you, thank you!"

Chapter 6

Bob Summers was on the phone when Jimmy approached his cubicle in the police station. Bob waved his friend to a seat, so Jimmy lowered himself onto a chair against the wall. He didn't have long to wait. Bob soon terminated the call and reached for a print-out to show to Jimmy.

"This Social Security list is all I have to show just now. As you can see, there are several men with the name Richard Nelson in the United States. I have circled this Richard U. Nelson, as I thought the U. might stand for Underwood. His date of birth is 6 June, 1945, which would make him twenty-one this year. Sounds about right, don't you agree?" asked Bob.

"Yes, Bob," agreed Jimmy, "that's probably our man. I am calling off the hounds, however, as I just finished talking with Richard in person.

"What! How did you find him? And so quickly!" exclaimed Bob.

"I didn't. God sent him to me. He gave a ride to a young woman who got off the bus in town and needed a way out to Lake Shore. He drove her out and parked right next to me. I saw him when I went to get in my car. He left in a hurry. I verified my suspicions with the young lady and followed him to town. He's working at SeaSpray Motors now, but he's ready to go home. He's agreed to give notice, pay his debts, and move his stuff back home."

"That's great, Jimmy! That's a much better ending than some of our hunts. I did not find his name on any police blotter in the area, so I assume the kid is clean," added Bob.

"I would guess that is true. I certainly appreciate your willingness to help me find this young man, Bob."

Jimmy put his hand to the chair seat, gave himself a push, and stood on his feet. As he offered his hand to Bob, he added, "Thank you again for your help. Like you, I am grateful to find him alive, well, and also more mature. He seems ready now to assume the responsibility given to him by his father's death."

Jalene tapped lightly on the door, heard Jimmy's booming "come in," and smiled as she greeted the big man behind the desk.

Jimmy stood to greet her. "Good to see you again, Miss Jalene." He gestured her to a chair near his desk. "I hope you and Miss Hester are having a good visit."

"Oh, yes! Dad and Mom took us out to dinner last evening. We all talked up a storm!" Her expression became serious as she spoke. "Jimmy, I've a question to ask you."

"Um," said Jimmy, "I didn't think this was a social call. What is your question?"

"Would I be permitted to live in the apartment with Hester?" she asked.

Jimmy leaned back in his chair and clasped his beefy hands over his ample stomach. "And just why would you want to do that, if I may ask?"

"She's alone. For the first time in her life, she is alone. She has spent her whole live caring for someone else. First, she cared for her parents, and then Grandmother Lena, and now she is alone. She can give you a long list of things she cannot do. But basically, she needs to be needed. I also live alone. My work is interesting, but I'm still alone. My friends are married and having children. I just do not fit in with my peers anymore. I am ready for a change. So I thought that if I could live with her, I could earn the living and pay the rent, and Hester could do what she does best: Cook, clean, and care for someone—me."

"Well, Miss Jalene, I think I understand what you're wanting, and I agree that Miss Hester needs to be needed. But about your living in the manor with her? Yes, you could as her guest until her lease expires. But you aren't eligible to sign a lease there, as you are too young. And I could not allow her to sign the papers knowing you were providing the means. That just wouldn't be honest, would it? I've a question for you. I am assuming you have a good job in Kansas City. If you were to come to Mozarkia, what would you plan to do for an income?"

"Yes, Jimmy, I do have a good job. I am a finance officer at the university. I am a certified public accountant, so I could hang out my shingle. I just thought some business might need an experienced bookkeeper and was leaving my place of employment up to the LORD," said Jalene.

"Hmmm," said Jimmy. "I take it that you like to work with numbers. Let me tell you something. When the LORD and I started this adventure after WorldWar II, I bought an acreage here along the lake. First thing we built was the lodge with one restaurant, Fisherman's Cove. We've added onto the lodge, added The Eagle's Nest Restaurant up on top, added the convention center and the Evergreen Room dining facility. All of this, plus the offices and Market Lane, is under one roof. How many people do you think it takes to keep just this building up and going day and night?"

"It takes a lot of people, Jimmy! Why, the restaurants, maintenance, maids, security, housekeeping, the lobby, the offices—it would take lots of people," replied Jalene.

"That's true. Then add to that number those at the marina, the stables and riding academy, the club house and golf course, the Cub House Day Care Center, and the other amenities as the gym, swimming pool, playground and such that make this a family resort, and you'll discover that I have a very large family indeed," said Jimmy. "They may all be employees, but they are my family."

"Yes, you do, Jimmy," agreed Jalene. "I can also see that though much comes in, very much is paid out, too."

"Lake Shore Resort started small, but it isn't small anymore. Each facility has its own office and keeps its own books balanced, but the master office is still the hub of the financial wheel. Keeping within the budget is necessary, you know."

"Each department at the university has to keep its books balanced, too. I work in the master office, so I know exactly what you are saying," added Jalene.

Jimmy glanced at his watch and apologetically said, "I'm sorry, Miss Jalene, but I have an appointment right soon. I need to head to town. To answer your question: After the lease has expired and if Miss Hester isn't able to pay the rent, then both of you would have to move. I'm sure the LORD has something for you. Just trust him," he said as he ushered Jalene to the door.

Chapter 7

Richard added the box to the others on the back seat of the blue Chevy and closed the door. He made one last trip to his former room in the boarding house to make sure he wasn't leaving anything. The dresser drawers and closet were empty. The bed was made. He had even taken extra care to make sure the spread was on straight and did not touch the floor anywhere. Satisfied, he stopped at Mrs. Smith's door in order to bid the kind lady farewell.

"Be careful driving home, Richard. If you ever need a room again, I hope I have one available," she beamed.

"Thank you," he replied.

Five minutes later, Richard was on the black-top highway headed north towards Lakeville. He had so many things to be thankful for; so much had happened the past two weeks.

He thought again of Jalene Anderson. She was so easy to talk with. She was very well dressed and quite pretty, too. But what he remembered was the compassion in her voice and those green eyes. She did know the feeling of being alone. It was bad enough to lose his dad at eighteen, but to grow up without a mother? That would really be difficult!

He was thankful, too, for Jimmy Hilton. He was some man! His heart must be as big as his body. You'd never know by the way he dressed or acted or talked that he was a wealthy man. He was really interested in his "family," as he called his employees.

Having a car was a real blessing, for sure, and then to have the promise of a job at LS. That job would be really great! To assemble new motors was fine, but Richard liked the idea of determining what was wrong with a motor and then fixing it. That was the challenge he anticipated!

The last promise Jimmy made was the most unexpected: "Richard," Jimmy had said, "after your sister is graduated in mid-May, you bring your family with you when you return to Lake Shore. You can live in The Village since you will be an employee."

He was glad he had called his mother. She had been as thrilled to hear his voice as he was to hear hers. It was a relief for each of them to cry together. He knew that right now his mother was watching for his return home. All he'd said was he would be driving a blue car.

It was his! The first car he had ever owned! Jimmy had insisted that Richard's name be on the title. Richard was determined to pay Jimmy every single dollar he owed him.

Richard felt the tears coming again. He spotted a lane off in the trees, pulled off into the shade, and cut the engine. "LORD, you've done so much for me. I am so grateful for all you have given me and provided for me. When I turned my back on you and Mom, I was miserable. I have learned so much. Thank you for being patient with me; for not turning away from me. You believed in me. Now, I believe in you, LORD, more than ever. Continue to bless Mom, Rosie, and me. Lead me daily, LORD, as I learn to be the head of the family. I hope you won't think it as being selfish on my part, but if you are willing, allow me to see that young lady again."

Richard dried his eyes, started the car, and backed out of

the lane and onto the road. He glanced at his watch. In less than ten minutes he would be home.

As Richard slowed to make the turn, he read the sign:

LAKEVILLE
Population 473

He started down the main street towards the business district, but he turned left at the bank onto a residential street. He wondered how many times he'd turned this corner: Walking, on his bike, in a car, and a few times at the wheel of the family car. A host of memories rolled across his mind like an endless movie. At one time, he could have named the occupants of each house on the street.

The Foster house seemed to be vacant. The shrubs were not trimmed, nor had the grass been mowed. He wondered about Johnny. They had had so much fun growing up.

When he reached the Nelson house, Richard drove off the street onto the graveled area he and his dad had made for a parking space. He turned off the engine and just sat there.

The house was a plain frame box with a porch across the front. A walk led to the front door. Originally, the house had had four rooms: A front room, a kitchen, and two bedrooms. After the war, the Nelsons had added a long room across the entire back. Right behind the kitchen was the bathroom and an area for Mom's Maytag washing machine and the rinse tubs. "Not fancy," Martha had said, "but better than Grandma's rub board." At the other end of the addition was Richard's room.

Behind the house and entered from the alley was a shed. It did not house the family car. Rather, it was William's shop. He had his tools in there, and that is where he worked on cars. Richard had spent many hours in that shed with his dad, watching, learning, and doing mechanical chores.

Everything was the same, yet not the same. Being away three years made him feel almost like a stranger. Yet he felt at peace to be home again. He saw a slight movement of the curtain at the front window and knew his mother was inside watching and waiting.

"LORD, thank you. Help me to do what is right," he prayed as he exited the car.

Chapter 8

Hester heard the telephone ring, laid aside her Bible, and went to answer the phone. "Hello," she said.

"Hester, this is Jalene. I'm so excited! I just had to call you!"

"Why, what has happened?" she inquired.

"God has answered my prayer, Hester! I just got off the phone with Jimmy Hilton. He called me to offer me a job at Lake Shore. One of his accountants has been called into service, and Jimmy offered me that position."

"That sounds nice—"

"But there's more, Hester," Jalene interrupted. "Since I'll be an employee, I am eligible to live in The Village. You can live there with me. Isn't that wonderful!"

"Yes, I guess. Just slow down, honey, and tell me again. These old ears just do not hear as fast as you are talking."

"Oh, I am sorry, Hester. I am just excited! Before I came back to Kansas City last month, I had a talk with Jimmy. I learned that I could stay with you for a short time as a guest like I did during spring break. But I could not move in to live with you, especially if I paid the rent. That just would not be honest. Jimmy asked me a whole bunch of questions: Why did I want to move down here? How did I plan to earn my way? What was I qualified to do? Things like that. I told him where

I worked and what I did here. I also told him I was leaving where I'd work up to the LORD. Jimmy just called me. One of his accountants has been called up to go to Vietnam. Jimmy offered me the position. And like I said, as an employee of Lake Shore, I would be eligible to live in The Village, and you could live there with me. You and I would be a family. This is the answer to our prayers, Hester. Isn't the LORD good?"

"Yes, he is. Now when will all of this take place, Jalene?" asked Hester.

"I have already given notice here at the university. My contract ends May 31, but I still have another week of vacation time due me. I'll notify my apartment manager that I'll be out by the end of May. I can get all my stuff in a car. Guess that's one advantage for living in a furnished apartment. I am expecting Mother to drive up to help me move when the time comes." Jalene paused a moment, then said, "Hester, does this sound good to you? I do not know when your lease is up, but God does. I have a feeling He's worked all of these details just for us. You won't need to do much packing, and I'll be there to help you. Tell me how you feel about this, Hester."

"I don't really know how I feel about all of this. I need some time to digest it all. I am relieved and grateful to you and Jimmy for how the LORD uses others to take care of me. I have tried not to worry, to just trust God. I find myself saying time and time again, LORD, now what? That seems to be my plea," said Hester.

"We shall continue to pray that we will follow him, Hester. Just wanted you to know what seems to be working out for us. I love you, Hester. Bye, now," said Jalene.

Hester put the phone in its cradle and sat down in Uncle

Will's chair. Though she had used it many years now because it had an attached arm on a hinge that she could fold across her lap to use as a writing desk, she still thought of the chair as Uncle Will's. It had been made for him to be his desk while he graded his math papers as he sat by the fire. Hester used the chair when she wrote in her journal. She had a floor lamp at her shoulder and a small bookcase nearby where she kept her few books and her journals.

Picking up her pen, she opened her journal to add the information from Jalene's phone call. Finishing that, she walked out on the balcony, stood at the railing, and prayed.

"Here I am again, LORD. I am 64 years old, and all I know to do is to cook and clean and care for others. Is that what you want me to do now—to keep house for Jalene? I know I cannot stay here in the manor. I have no means to afford this. I do thank you for allowing me to live here these past months and to enjoy the view from this balcony. It has been balm for my soul. I have enjoyed your presence and the beauty of your handiwork every day. To watch winter change into spring reminded me of the change you made in me when I gave you my old self and you made me a new creation in Christ Jesus. I thank you, LORD, for what Jesus did for me on the cross. I thank you that he rose from the dead to show me that my turn will come some day. I know that when I leave this earthly home I will go to be with you. I thank you for that. You have brought me this far. Now what? You know what you have planned for me. Grant me patience to wait. I trust you, LORD, and want to follow wherever you want me to go. I love you, LORD."

Richard Nelson did not have any problem convincing his

mother and sister to leave Lakeville. His parents had bought "the little white box" when they were first married. They had added to the house after they added two children to the family. They had built a loving family on their faith in God. William's sudden death had been a shock and difficult to bear, but Martha and her daughter had weathered their loss—without Richard.

They had many happy memories of their years in Lakeville. But the time had come to move on and to trust God for the adventure.

Richard listed the house for sale. He got boxes from the grocery store for packing books, dishes, and such stuff. They sorted their belongings and decided what to sell and what to move. Each day was busy and tiring. Yet an element of expectation was also there.

By graduation time, Roseann was able to walk on her own. It was a bittersweet event for her when she left the school that night. The class members were happy to graduate, yet they knew this would be their last time to be together. Some were going into service, some to work, and some off to college in the fall. Roseann hugged her girlfriends and wiped her tears as she made her way to the car and the forthcoming relocation of her family.

Jimmy had told Richard to contact the man at the furniture store in Mozarkia. He had a large boxy truck that was just right for hauling furniture and two men able to do just that. Richard called and they set a date.

When that day arrived, the Nelsons were ready. They loaded up, and the move was made without mishap.

Richard settled his family in a three-bedroom house on Woodfern Lane at the end nearest to the lake. Just across the way was a park with a Victorian gazebo. He thought his sister would like that—he assumed she still read a lot. His being away those three years had caused him to lose track of her. He was eager to get unloaded, pay the men, and be busy setting up in their new location. He was also eager to report to work on the morrow.

Chapter 9

Hester took her journals and her few books from the box and placed them back in the book case. Moving there from the apartment had gone quite well. Both Jalene and Ruth had helped her to pack. She had appreciated that. Charles had contacted the man at the furniture store who had a truck equipped to move furniture and two men who did that. Charles had hired them to move Hester's things. They moved it all this morning in one trip.

The men had put the round oak table and chairs in the dining area and her oak bed and dresser in the front bedroom. Aunt Lena's Jenny Lind bed was in the other bedroom for Jalene.

In the living area were the couch, Uncle Will's chair, the floor lamp, and Hester's small bookcase. The lone begonia to survive the move from Kansas City last year was on its stand in front of the picture window. Jalene's contribution to the living area was a black and white television. Hester couldn't explain how a telephone or a radio could send voices. But pictures? That was definitely beyond her!

Ruth was in the kitchen. Hester could hear her putting away the cookware. Jalene was at work in her new location, an office on the mezzanine at the lodge not far from Jimmy's office. She promised to show it to Hester after she got well settled.

Hester paused to look around her. Woodfern Lane ran back into the trees that grew along the shore of Lake Mozarkia. Only the two houses on the end of the drive were near the lake. The ones next to them and all the rest stretched back into the woods the full length of the lane. Jimmy said there was a cul-de-sac at that end.

The house across the street was a three-bedroom house, as was the house next door. This house had two bedrooms. The two floor plans were alternated all the way down the street, Jimmy had told her. They were all on one floor with an attached garage.

But what had really appealed to Hester was the park across the way next to the lake. She had noticed it right off when Charles and Ruth drove her over there the first time. The park had trees, flowers, walks, and a white Victorian gazebo. Hester was anticipating the opportunity to take her Bible and to absorb the beauty of the lake from that gazebo.

"You have that box empty, I see," said Ruth as she entered the room. "I'll put this empty one in the garage and bring you another one to unpack." Returning with the filled box, Ruth set it on the floor then she sat on the couch. "I think you will enjoy living here, Hester."

"I think so, too," agreed Hester. "I'll miss the view from the balcony, but I've been thinking about that little park over there and that gazebo. It must have a beautiful view of its own."

"You're probably right. Are you ready for lunch? I have something prepared for us, if you are," asked Ruth.

"That sounds good, and smells good, too. Smells like biscuits," said Hester.

"It is," agreed Ruth. "I fixed a quickie lunch—a favorite of my mother, if I remember correctly: The one with scrambled eggs, bacon, hominy, and hot biscuits. I didn't find any bacon, but it will be good, anyway," she added.

"I hadn't thought about being hungry, but I am ready to stop this for a little while," Hester said as she followed Ruth to the kitchen. After washing her hands, she joined Ruth at the table. The two women held hands while Ruth expressed their thanks.

After they had eaten and cleaned up the kitchen, Ruth said she needed to go check on Charles. "We have the kitchen in some semblance of order. The beds are ready to use, so you can relax and rest this afternoon, Hester. I'll come back in the morning."

Hester thanked Ruth for all she had done and added, "I think I shall take my Bible and go over to that gazebo. I can hardly wait to learn what I can see from there! I just know God has a vista of beauty for me to behold."

After Ruth left, Hester stood in front of her mirror. She used her wet hands to smooth down her hair, making sure no loose hairs were outside her bun. Satisfied, she picked up her Bible, walked out to Woodfern Lane, crossed Village Avenue, and entered the park. Reaching the gazebo, she paused to look around. From there she could see that the park was laid out like a wagon wheel with the gazebo as the hub. The footpaths were the spokes, and inside the sections were the flower beds. The gazebo sat on the crest of the area. Beyond it the ground sloped downhill towards Lake Mozarkia, making the park larger than she thought. From the house, Hester had not been able to see any farther than the gazebo. Inside it was a five-sided table and benches.

The view from there was lovely! Everything—the sky, the

lake, the trees, and the flowers—made a beautiful scene. Hester put her Bible on the table and went exploring. She wanted to see what was beyond the bushes at the base of the slope. She carefully walked down the path to discover the bushes were lilacs. They must have been lovely just a few weeks ago when they were in full bloom, she thought. Following the path that made the rim of the wheel, Hester came to an opening to the lake side of the bushes.

On the other side, Hester found a gravel beach that separated the water from the vegetation along the shore. A few benches were in the grass alongside the beach. A teen-aged girl was sitting on one of the benches. She had an opened book in her lap, but she was staring out across the lake. The girl turned her head when she heard Hester approaching.

"Good afternoon," said Hester. "I do hope I am not intruding."

"Oh, no," said the girl. "I'm just daydreaming."

"Hester walked closer. "I'm Hester Wirth. I've just moved here today. I could hardly wait to come explore this lovely place. It's larger than I thought, but so pretty."

"I'm Roseann Nelson. We just moved here last Monday. I've been helping Mom unpack. She said she needed to rest, so I decided to come here to let her take a nap if she can. Won't you sit down?" she invited.

"Thank you. I live in the first house on the left," Hester stated. "Which one is your house?"

"We live in the first house on the right. We are just across the street from each other! Do you live alone?" she inquired.

"No, I have a companion who works here at Lake Shore. We are cousins, but it's rather complicated. Guess the easiest way to say it would be that her grandmother and my mother were sisters. I was her grandmother's housekeeper and caretaker for over twenty years in Kansas City. We—Aunt Lena and I—came to the Manor last year. But I couldn't stay in the Manor after Aunt Lena died," Hester explained.

"I'm sorry. We sorta had to move, too. My dad was killed three years ago. Mom and I toughed it out until I finished high school. Then my brother got a job here, and we were able to live in The Village. This is a lovely place, but I am so lonely. I don't know anyone. I don't have anything to do. I am so lonely..." She began to cry.

In an instant, Hester reached for the crying girl and pulled her into her arms. "Shh," she crooned, "I know how that feels. I'm alone, too. My parents are both gone. I've never married. I don't have any skills, so nobody would hire me. All I know to do is cook, clean house, and care for others. I know God cares for me because he continually provides for me. Let's go up to the gazebo. There's a table up there and shade. I have something I want to read to you."

Hester and Roseann walked up to the gazebo. After they were seated, Hester opened her Bible to the Psalms and began to read the twenty-third: "The LORD is my shepherd." She paused. "Do you know what a shepherd is, Roseann?"

"Not really. They raise sheep. I know that much," she answered.

"Sheep are interesting animals. They require water to drink and green grass to eat. The water has to be still, quiet—not a moving stream or rushing river. And they must be led. You cannot drive sheep like cattle or horses. You have to go in front to lead them. Because the sheep trust the shepherd, they will follow him. Sheep trust the shepherd to lead them where there is food and water," related Hester.

"That's interesting," Roseann said. "Is there more?"

"Yes, look at verse four. Even though the path may be in

a ravine, by cliffs and dark places, the sheep trust the shepherd to lead them through. They know he has a rod and staff to scare off wolves or even lift out one that falls over the edge. The shepherd loves and cares for his sheep, and they trust him to provide that care," continued Hester.

"That is so interesting!" exclaimed Roseann. "I've never heard that before."

"There is more, Roseann. Like David, the man who wrote this, I can say the LORD is my shepherd. I am one of his sheep. He loves me, cares for me, and sees that I have food and drink, and that I am protected from the wolves. All because I trust him, try to follow his leading, and I know he will not lead me astray."

"Let me tell you more about me. I'm just a plain country girl who never went off to college or to work away from home. I don't even know how to drive a car. I stayed home to be the housekeeper while Mama took care of Papa. He was laid up with terrible pain. He had fallen under the wheel of a wagon load of hay sometime before. After Papa died, and then Mama, I was all alone. My mother's sister invited me to come to Kansas City to live with her. She was a widow with two married daughters. Then the war came along. One daughter's husband was killed at Pearl Harbor; the other's husband was sent overseas. Both girls came home to be with their mother. The pregnant daughter gave birth to twin girls. I was busy keeping house, doing the cooking, the laundry, etc., while the others took care of the babies."

"You see, Roseann," Hester explained, "Aunt Lena thought she was helping out her niece to offer me a place to live, and she really did. God knew that Aunt Lena would need me in the years to come. God knew that Louise would deliver twins. He also knew that Louise would not survive the train wreck and what would happen to her little girl. After that, it was three women and one little girl until Charles came home after the war. In time, he claimed his daughter and married his wife's sister. God used Jimmy Hilton in order for Charles and his missing daughter to be united. It was Jimmy who mentioned a business in town that was for sale. Charles purchased it and moved to Mozarkia. Then Aunt Lena and I came to the Manor. Can you see, Roseann, that when we are in tune with God and allow him to lead, he will lead? Like obedient sheep, we need to trust him and just follow."

"Wow! What an interesting story! Sounds like something out of a novel!" she exclaimed.

"I hope you can see why I feel so alone at times. But I know, too, that God is still in charge. After my parents died, I had to sell the farm and dispose of much of our stuff. That was hard to do. I think I am stronger for having done it. I know God was with me, too. So whatever experience you have had to come through, that is what it is—an experience—and you did come through it. Learn from it. Anticipate the next experience as an adventure. That's enough about me. What about you? Do you want to go to college? What do you like to do? What do you want to be?"

"Really, Miss Hester," said Roseann, "I don't know. I didn't excel in anything in particular. I did sing in the mixed chorus at school. My sophomore year, I tried running but I dropped out after Dad's death. I'm not especially interested in home ec, science, or math. I did make decent grades. I do like to read. I do a lot of that! My cousin Sarah works at the Cub House. She likes little children. She's asked me to visit her at work. But I've never been around little children much. I have no younger siblings, and I never did any baby sitting.

Just didn't have the desire to do that. I'm just a quiet person," finished Roseann.

"What's the book you have there?" asked Hester.

"I found this in Richard's stuff," she said, showing the book to Hester. "It's *Thunder Road*, about car racing. I don't find it interesting at all."

"What kind of books do you like?" asked Hester.

"I prefer historical novels. My friends in high school read boy-meets-girl romances. You can read a dozen of them and not learn a thing. Same plot, just different characters in a different setting. I like to learn something when I read. I don't mind some romance, but I like the story to tell about events that really happened."

"Roseann, have you ever been in a large library?" asked Hester.

"No, ma'am," she replied, "just the one in our school at Lakeville."

"Would you like to see what goes on in a large library? To see what kinds of resources are there? Since you like books so well, you might like to become a librarian. I know one of the librarians at Middleton College. I'm sure I could get her to give you a tour."

"Really? I think that sounds great!" exclaimed Roseann. "When do you think she might do that?"

"I'll check into that," said Hester, rising from the stone bench. "I've sat here long enough. I have enjoyed our conversation, Roseann."

"So have I!" said Roseann. "May I ask you something?"

"Of course."

"I'd like for Sarah to meet you. She and Aunt Lydia are to have dinner with us Sunday. Could Sarah and I come here Sunday afternoon to visit with you?" asked Roseann.

"I think that sounds lovely. I'll look forward to it. Bye now."

Chapter 10

On their first Sunday in The Village, Jalene announced she was going to town to attend worship services with her dad and mom.

"Come go with me, Hester," she invited.

Hester declined, saying, "Thanks for the invitation, but I'll go over to the chapel for worship. After your grandmother's death, I rode the shuttle bus from the Manor and got acquainted with some of the other regulars. You go on to town, enjoy your time with your folks, and don't worry about me. I'll be fine. Besides, I am to meet Roseann and her cousin this afternoon, so stay as long as you wish."

Hester walked to the chapel. She was impressed again by the simplicity of its structure. Made of stone, the building had skylights designed to allow the beauty of the outdoors to blend with the interior. A circular window behind the pulpit was the focal point. Its muted greens, gold, and blues emphasized the red cross in its center.

Jimmy had told Hester about the Christian banker from Chicago who had come to Lake Shore when the resort was new. The banker had liked the Christian atmosphere and that no alcohol was permitted. He had suggested to Jimmy that he needed to provide a place of worship that would be convenient for his patrons and his employees. The Long Shore Chapel was built soon after that.

Hester liked Chaplain Davidson. Although he was about her age, he had a good rapport with the youth and the children who attended, as well.

She didn't linger after the service. She was eager to eat her lunch, clean up the kitchen, and be at the gazebo when the girls came.

Hester was sitting in the gazebo with her back to the street, facing the lake and drinking in the view beyond the park, when she heard giggling and knew the girls were coming.

Roseann spoke to Hester. "Thank you for coming. This is my cousin Sarah Carson. Our mothers are sisters."

Roseann was lithe and slender, whereas Sarah was a little heavier, though not chubby. She was just more developed and a little older. Sarah had bright red hair and freckles that seemed to dance around her dimples when she smiled. And Sarah did a lot of that.

Hester said with a smile, "I am happy to meet you, Sarah. Roseann and I had such a nice visit the other day. I suppose she has told you all about me. She said you worked at the Cub House. How long have you worked for Jimmy?"

"I signed up when I was thirteen, but I couldn't be employed until I was sixteen. And then, I could only work the short shift at the childcare center. That's the five-to-eight shift. A whole bunch of us girls work that shift. We are the scrub crew. We sterilize and sanitize every toy, utensil, table, chair—the whole place—every evening. We each are assigned a certain room or area to work. Our supervisor has everything ready by five. We come, get our bucket of solution, and go to our places to do our job. We know the health of the children depends on our doing our job well.

"I'm sure Jimmy pays you for your services, right?" inquired Hester.

"Yes, we are paid. In addition, we are earning credits towards college scholarships. We also know that there are lots of others on Jimmy's list who want our jobs. That keeps us doing our best. It is really a black mark against you in this area if you are fired by Jimmy Hilton. Also, it is an excellent recommendation if you can have years of working for him. I have worked for Jimmy for four years."

"I take it you like your work," commented Hester.

"I am not on a scrub crew now. I liked that, but I like my present job better. When I learned that Mrs. Williams was going to need a replacement while she was out for her surgery, I asked Jimmy if I could go to full-time on the day shift. My housekeeping chores are different, but I get to be around the children," she added.

"Oh, so you are the one who had a reason to want that job!" Hester said. "Jimmy offered me that position, but God wanted me to decline. That freed Jimmy to allow you to take it," she explained.

"Yes, well, Mother and I decided I could lay out of college this term in order for me to work days," Sarah explained.

"He said that person had a pressing need. I surely hope this takes care of it and you are able to return to college," said Hester.

"Well, to be honest," Roseann said, "the need was us. Mother and I were having it really tough until Aunt Lydia and Sarah began sending us some cash. My dad's insurance money had run out. Mother is an excellent seamstress, but there just wasn't that much business in Lakeville for her to make a living. We have hopes of things improving now that my brother has come home," finished Roseann.

"We hope so, too," Hester said, patting Roseann's hand. "Sarah, what are you studying to become?" asked Hester.

"I love little children! I want to get a degree in elementary education," Sarah said. "I'll need to transfer to a larger college to do that. The community college in Mozarkia is just a glorified high school. I'd like to go to Middleton College."

"Hmmm," said Hester. "Maybe I can help there. I know some people on the staff at Middleton. I've already promised Roseann to arrange for her a tour of the library. Maybe you can go along to see about a scholarship or even learn how to enter one of their work study programs."

"That sounds great! Until Mrs. Williams is able to be back at work, I cannot go during the week. But she may be back soon. She visited us at the Cub House just this week and said she hopes the doctor will give her permission to return to work shortly."

"I shall call Janelle to set up a time. Oh, Janelle is Jalene's twin sister. She is one of the librarians at Middleton. Her husband is a member of the music faculty. A trip to Middleton College would acquaint you with the campus and allow you to see what the college has to offer," Hester said.

Picking up her Bible, Hester turned to Sarah. "Have you ever heard of the word 'metamorphosis'?"

"Yes, I have," Sarah replied. "It has to do with the cycle of life of a butterfly. It's amazing! One of the boys in my high school science class found a chrysalis on a bush. He broke off the branch to bring it to school. Mr. Brown showed it to us and put the branch on top of the book case. We sorta forgot about it. On one of those days the next spring when we had the windows open 'cause it was so warm, one of the girls spoke up. She didn't even raise her hand to get permission to speak. She just blurted out, 'Look!' We saw this thing clinging to the side of the bookcase. It was alive! We just sat there watching it. Little by little, it slowly unfurled its wings and opened up to be a beautiful Luna moth. It was amazing!" finished Sarah.

"Did you know that transformation is in the Bible?" asked Hester.

"No," said Sarah.

"Show us, Hester," added Roseann.

So Hester opened her Bible to Romans, chapter twelve, and began to read: "I beseech you therefore, brethren, by the mercies of God, that ye present your bodies a living sacrifice, holy acceptable unto God, which is your reasonable service. And be not conformed to this world; but be ye transformed by the renewing of your mind, that ye may prove what is that good, and acceptable, and perfect will of God." (Romans 12:1-2)

Hester explained, "As in everything we read, we need to know the meaning of the words in order to understand what the writer is trying to say. Watch the meaning develop as I explain these words and phrases. *Brethren:* Paul wrote this to those who believed that Jesus is God's son and chose to follow him. *Living sacrifice:* means complete devotion to God. A person who desires to allow God to be in control of his life daily, sacrifices or gives up himself to be used by God. *Reasonable service:* That is what is expected of us as believers. When we consider what Jesus did for us by dying on the cross, can we do less than our best for him? *Not conformed:* To conform means to take the shape of, as water conforms to the shape and size of the container. Believers are in the world, but we are not to be like the world and live like unbelievers. Rather, we are to *be transformed:* Paul used that word 'metamorphosis.' It means to 'have a form altered' or to be changed. As believers, we have, by God's grace, been born again. We have been changed to become new creations in Christ. *Renewing of your mind:* Since we have given ourselves to him, even our minds, he wants us to see through new eyes and think like him. *To prove* is to test, in order to find out what is good and acceptable to God.

"Whee!" said Sarah. "I didn't know all of that was in those two verses!"

"Ah, but there is so much in God's word! We can never learn it all," said Hester.

When Jalene returned that afternoon, she could see Hester and the two girls in the gazebo. She strolled over to join them. "Hope I am not interrupting," she said.

"Of course not," said Hester. "Jalene, I'd like you to meet our neighbor Roseann Nelson and her cousin Sarah Carson. Sarah has been working at the Cub House while Mrs. Williams is on sick leave due to her recent surgery. This is my cousin, Jalene Anderson."

Jalene seated herself next to Hester with her back to the street. Thus she was surprised several minutes later when a male voice behind her said, "Sarah, Aunt Lydia is ready to leave."

The two girls quickly jumped to their feet. They politely bade Hester and Jalene bye, thanked Hester for the Bible lesson, and departed.

Willing herself to slowly exhale the breath she had been holding, Jalene turned to face the voice she remembered so well.

"Richard?" she asked. "Is that really you?"

"Jalene!" he exclaimed. "I've been hoping I'd get to see you again!"

"Hmmm," said Hester. "I take it that you two have already met somewhere?"

"He was the young man who drove me out to Lake Shore on my spring break," explained Jalene.

"I'm Richard Nelson. Roseann is my sister," he said.

"I'm happy to meet you, Richard. I am enjoying your sister's friendship. But I have sat long enough." She rose stiffly from the stone bench. "I think I'll go back home." She picked up her Bible and left the gazebo.

Richard took Jalene's hand, pulled her to her feet, and indicated the path down towards the lake. They found a bench where they could sit and talk.

"Now," said Richard, "catch me up. Where did you come from? I thought you were in Kansas City!"

Jalene told Richard about her concern for Hester, her talk with Jimmy, her giving notice on faith, Jimmy's phone call, and their moving to Woodfern Lane in The Village. "The LORD just put it all together. He's so good! Your turn."

Richard related his first conversation with Jimmy, calling his mother, buying the car, giving notice, and going home. He also told how God had led them in selling the house, getting moved, and his new job. "I have my own bay at the marina. I think I'll put up a sign, RUN. That's my initials: Richard Underwood Nelson. Maybe I should let the sign say IT RUNS. I just want my customers to know engines I work on do run.

"Jalene," he continued, "I learned a lot those years I was on my own. I learned a greater appreciation for my family and for God. I played the fool when I turned my back on God. I am so thankful he did not turn his back on me. I have prayed every day since I met you that if it were his will, God would permit me to see you again. I have not been able to forget you, Jalene. When you turned around and I discovered that other person was you, it hit me like a ton of bricks: God answered my prayers! For a moment I couldn't say anything. I'm so thankful! I just don't know what to do!"

"I know," Jalene said. She took Richard's two hands in hers and bowed her head: "LORD, we thank you for bringing Richard and me to this place. We know you love us and have cared for us and have brought us together for some purpose. We ask that you will lead us; that we can enjoy being friends and becoming better acquainted. May our relationship honor your name for Jesus' sake. Amen."

And Richard added, "Amen"

"Thank you, Jalene. I wanted to express my thanks. Guess I was a bit afraid of how you might feel if I did. You have the same feelings as I do. I am glad! Very glad!

And just think, you live across the street! Not exactly the girl next door but close to it. I hope I don't make a pest of myself to Hester, but I intend to see you often. OK?" he asked.

"I'd like that," agreed Jalene, "very much."

Hester fixed herself a glass of iced tea and went to the living room to sit on the soft couch for a spell. She decided to call Janelle, who was pleased to hear her voice.

"Janelle, this is Hester. Before you ask, we are all fine. I just called to ask a favor of you."

"You know I'll do whatever I can, Hester. What is your wish?" she asked.

"I have become acquainted with two girls here. Roseann just graduated from high school, and her cousin Sarah has been attending the local college. Roseann is a quiet person and likes to read. I'd like for her to have a chance to see your library. She might like to become a librarian herself some-day. Her cousin Sarah is fond of little children and wants to obtain a degree in elementary education. Both girls need to learn about scholarships and the work study program offered at Middleton College," said Hester.

"When do they want to come?" asked Janelle.

"Whenever it would be convenient for you, Janelle. I am hoping that Ruth might drive them up. If you select a week-day, I rather doubt that Jalene could come," Hester said.

"It would almost have to be during the week, as the of-fices are closed on Saturdays. I'd be delighted to give the girls a tour! Tell you what; I'll send my work schedule to Ruth. She can choose what day fits her schedule. Once we get that settled, I think the rest will fall into place. How does that sound?" asked Janelle.

"That sounds fine with me. And thank you, Janelle. These are both nice girls who are wanting to become women of worth," Hester added. "Bye."

Hester finished her tea and went to the kitchen. She rinsed out her glass and set it on the counter by the sink. She returned to the living room to sit in Uncle Will's chair.

Pulling up the arm, she opened her journal to write the happenings of the day. So much had taken place: Worship at the chapel, her visit with the girls in the gazebo, and the Bible lesson. She had thought she'd read another Psalm, but God seemed to want those two verses from Romans. The experience Sarah related had really added to the explanation. The LORD is surely at work! And Roseann's brother was the young man Jalene had met last March. Now, I wonder what the LORD has up his sleeve, she thought. I do so hope Ruth will be available to take the girls to Middleton. I know Jalene would like to go, too, but I'll just have to leave that up to the LORD. It's time for me to prepare supper.

Chapter 12

After their day's work and the evening meal was finished, Richard and Jalene would meet at the gazebo to spend the evening together. They went for long walks up and down the many hiking trails and pathways through the woods. They went horseback riding, even to Summit Point to view Lake Shore Resort from its highest park. Often they would sit on a bench beyond the lilacs to study their Bibles together and pray. Wherever they were or whatever they were doing, they talked and talked.

One evening, Richard took Jalene out on the lake. They went past the island to a small private beach. There they sat to watch the sun go down over the water. A few puffy white clouds floated across the blue sky. But as time passed, the clouds reflected the rainbow of colors from the setting sun. It was beautiful!

They never ran out of things to talk about. They had so many memories of growing up to tell each other. They had testimonies of how God had blessed their families. The more they talked and the more they learned about each other, the stronger their friendship became.

One evening when they returned to the gazebo, Richard pulled Jalene into his arms and just held her close. "This feels so right," he said over the top of her head as he gazed out towards the lake. "I want to hold you; to take care of you. I just want to be with you forever." He lifted her chin to look straight into her green eyes. "I love you, Jalene Anderson."

Before Jalene could say anything, Richard pressed his lips on her mouth, gently at first, then with ardor. With her heart pounding, Jalene returned his kiss.

Then, gently pulling back, Jalene looked at the face that had come to mean so much to her. "I love you, too, Richard. I really do. I feel God has brought us together. And as much as I'd like to walk into the sunset with you, I can't, not now. So please, don't ask"

Surprised, Richard asked, "What are you saying?"

"I'm saying that you have a commitment to your mother and sister, and I have one with Hester. We cannot walk away from them right now. We'll just have to continue as we are until the LORD shows us how to cope with our responsibilities. We'll just have to trust him and wait until he says the time is right," she said.

"May I ask your father for your hand? I want you to be mine! I want to put a ring on your finger! I want everyone to know I have found the girl of my dreams! I want—"

Jalene laid her forefinger on his lips. "Shhh. Be patient, my love. Think for a minute. You have expenses each month. You're still paying Jimmy for the car. Your salary is not all that much, Richard. You may start saving to buy a ring someday. We must wait—"

"I don't want to wait!" he interrupted.

"I know. But we must wait. God knows how we feel. We must trust him and allow him to be in charge. Just trust him. Our day will come. He knows best. Remember, I waited eighteen years to see my sister."

"I don't want to wait any eighteen years!" he stated firmly.

Richard pulled her close to him as they sat on the bench, leaving his arm about her waist. Closing his eyes, Richard prayed: "Lord, I thank you for Jalene. I thank you for bringing us together. I thank you for the love that fills me when I am with her. I pray, Lord, for patience and the hope that one day you will permit us to marry. And, Lord, we want your blessings on our love; that it will remain strong, and that we may keep ourselves pure. Help us to continue to provide for those in our care. Just lead us, Lord." Richard paused.

Jalene added: "This is our prayer, in Jesus' name. Amen"

Chapter 13

On a warm July morning, Ruth took Roseann and Sarah to Middleton.

Hester was sitting in Uncle Will's chair, writing the grocery list for Jalene when Ruth arrived across the street to pick up the girls. The girls came out, but Roseann went back into the house. Guess she forgot something, thought Hester. But when she returned, Roseann was wearing a summer dress, not the shirt and shorts as before.

Hmmm, thought Hester. I hadn't remembered, but shorts are not permitted on campus at Middleton College. I'm glad Ruth knew to have her change. She might have been terribly embarrassed.

"Thank you, LORD, for Ruth: For her willingness to take the girls, her understanding of the rules, and her desire to make this a happy experience for Roseann and Sarah. Give them safety, LORD, as they travel. Give them a day to observe, to learn, and to decide what they need to do to make of themselves the kind of women you desire. And LORD, thank you for Janelle and her willingness to use her day off to make some new friends. And bless Jalene, LORD. She wanted so much to be with them today. Give all of us the patience to allow you to lead; trusting you, like obedient sheep, because the shepherd knows what is best."

Hester, Martha, and Lydia had decided to have a picnic at the gazebo that evening. The girls could tell of their day's events just once and all would hear it the first telling.

Lydia and Martha chose to bring fried chicken and baked beans. The sisters would also contribute cake or cookies for dessert. Hester would supply the potato salad and some deviled eggs. She'd leave them in the refrigerator until the group was ready to eat, then Jalene could go get them.

Richard said he'd supply the soda pop. Jalene offered to bring paper plates and cups. Ruth had said they'd probably be back by 5:30 or so.

The group gathered at the gazebo, expecting a happy time together when the travelers returned. The pop was on ice in a foot tub. The paper plates and napkins were weighted down with the salt and pepper shakers. All the food was present except for the two items in Hester's refrigerator.

It was already 6:00, then 6:15 came and still no girls. Jalene was the first one to see Ruth's car about two blocks away. It was nearly 6:30 when they unloaded. Ruth apologized for the delay.

"It was all Karl's fault," said Sarah.

"Just sorta," agreed Roseann.

Ruth explained, "Janelle had hoped Karl would be able to meet the girls, but he'd had a busy day with classes and private lessons. He was not able to meet with us. Finally, Janelle said he might have a break about 3:00, so we all went to the music building. He wasn't in his classroom, nor his office, nor his studio, so we were ready to come on home."

"That's when we heard the most beautiful music," chimed in Roseann. "It was coming from the recital hall. Janelle opened the door quietly. We all stepped inside and sat down in the dark. The only lights were up on the stage."

"And the longest piano I have ever seen!" added Sarah.

"And the man playing the piano was Karl. I don't know what he was playing, but it was beautiful! I just sat and watched his hands flow over the keys," continued Roseann.

"Janelle went down front to speak to him," Sarah said. "Then he called us to come, too. He was waiting for another pupil We were happy to see him in the lights. My, he's handsome!"

"And that is why we were later leaving Middleton than we had planned," concluded Ruth.

Hester suggested Ruth join them at their picnic, but she declined. "I need to get home to check on Charles. Those girls have so much to tell they won't have time to eat. Roseann, Sarah, thanks for a very enjoyable day. I appreciated the chance to spend some time with Janelle."

"Thank you for taking us," said Sarah.

"We appreciate your doing that," added Roseann.

After Ruth left and all the food was on the table, the group gathered around while Richard expressed thanks for the food, the safe trip, and the good fellowship coming up.

Hester's question: "Did you have any surprises?"

Roseann answered, "Yes, I was surprised to learn that shorts were not permitted on that campus. I was at first miffed because Ruth had me change clothes. Later, I was glad I had. Janelle took us to the Union for lunch. I would have really stuck out had I been wearing shorts among all those other girls."

Hester turned to Sarah and asked, "Did anything surprise you?"

"Yes, Janelle did. I knew she was Jalene's sister, and I may have heard that they were twins. I've known twins that looked somewhat alike, but these two girls are identical! I just didn't realize two people could be so much alike!" said Sarah.

"And remember," added Hester, "Jalene and Janelle were separated for eighteen years. They didn't grow up as sisters. That they even got reunited is a miracle."

"I'm glad I got to see the library," said Roseann. "It's big! It has stacks and stacks of books, and all kinds of resources, files, catalogues, and such to help one find whatever is needed. There are little rooms with a table and chair where one can go to study in private. Janelle told us about one night when she was a student that she had the late shift and was to lock up. She said she had turned the lights off-and-on to signal closing time and thought everyone was gone. She was making one last circuit to be sure lights were off in the restrooms when she saw a sliver of light shining under the door of one study room The student had fallen asleep with his head on his books. Had he awakened after she had locked up, he would have found total darkness."

"I got to see the Child Study Center," volunteered Sarah. "The children are all local pre-schoolers. Their parents are either on the college faculty/staff or they live near to the campus. Many of the workers are students taking courses to learn how to work with children that age. They were a lot of busy little people!"

"Janelle took us to the administration building where we filled out some pre-registration papers. They need a copy of our transcripts, our parents' signatures, and some other stuff before we can be accepted," explained Roseann.

"Like Roseann said earlier, we ate lunch in the Union. With so many lines to choose from and so many people, you'd think it would be hectic. Everyone seemed to know where to go for what. It really worked smoothly. When I saw how many people were there, I thought it would take a long time to get a tray filled. But we were in line, got our tray and our food, ate, and were back outside within thirty minutes. It took us twenty-five minutes in high school for less that two-hundred people. I was amazed!" said Sarah.

"The campus is really pretty," Roseann said. "Many of the sidewalks are like dual highways except the median is a flower bed. Janelle said the tulips and jonquils were very pretty last spring. She said she especially likes the fall, when the beds are filled with chrysanthemums. All colors of day lilies were in bloom, and some other plant that looks much like the one you have in your big window, Hester."

It had been an exciting day for them. Hester realized that neither girl had been that far from home before. They both seemed eager to get enrolled at Middleton College.

Chapter 14

A quick knock on the door caused Hester to look up from her journal. Through the window she could see Roseann and waved for her to come in.

Roseann burst into the room, waving a letter. "I got it, Hester! I got it! I've been accepted as a freshman at Middleton! I have room 324 in Rachel Hall. It opens for occupancy on August 25th. Classes begin on Monday, the 29th. My roommate is Lily Green, from Dogwood, Ark. That's only three weeks from now. I've lots to do! Just wanted you to know!"

And before Hester could say a word, Roseann was gone.

Whee! thought Hester. "Thank you, LORD"

Less than an hour later, Hester answered the phone. It was Sarah.

"Just wanted you to know, Hester, I've a letter from Middleton. I've been accepted as a sophomore."

"Glad to hear that, Sarah," commented Hester.

"I'm to live in Rachel Hall, room 126, and my roommate is Kathryn Smith from St. Joseph, Missouri. Yes, I have talked to Roseann. We are in the same dorm, but all freshmen are up on the third floor. They have their own monitors and own house rules. She read them to me. Classes start in three weeks. This letter does not say anything about work study, finances, or such," said Sarah.

"That will come from the business office, Sarah. This letter just told you about your living accommodations. I'm glad you were accepted. Thanks for telling me," said Hester.

Hester called Jalene at work. "Just wanted you to know that the girls have both been accepted at Middleton College. They are in the same dorm, but Roseann is up on third floor since she's a freshman."

"Great!" said Jalene. "Thanks for the call."

Hester finished writing in her journal and went to check her mailbox. She had a paper tube, which she took to the kitchen. She used her paring knife to slit the tube, and she unrolled a copy of the *Middleton Journal*. Janelle must have sent this for some reason, she thought. Returning to the living room, Hester read various headlines and a few items. Several concerned the fall opening of the college, their first athletic events, and such. Since she didn't find anything about Karl or Janelle, she decided to pass it along to the family across the street.

When Jalene came home from work, she spoke to Hester and said she was going over to see Roseann a minute. "Take that newspaper that came today, please. Those items about activities at the college might be of interest to them." An item in the classifieds:

> WANTED: Seamstress, must have experience doing alterations and sewing on exquisite fabrics. BRIDES' BOUTIQUE, west side of Square, Middleton." Hester did not see it, but Martha did.

That's just what I need, she thought. I could earn enough

to care for myself and apply some on Roseann's college fees. I could make more in a college town than here.

Martha called the shop. After her conversation with the lady in charge, Martha began getting her own things ready to go to Middleton for a month's probation for the position. She packed her suitcase with plans to stay in Middleton when they took Roseann in a few weeks.

When Martha announced to her family that night what she was planning to do, Roseann was excited. "Oh, Mother! I think that would be great to have you live in the same town!"

"What do you think, Richard?" asked his mother.

"I don't know what to think. I knew having Roseann away would make it different here at home with just the two of us, but I had not thought what you would have to do while I was at work. I can see that you probably wouldn't take in much sewing around here. If you were to get the position—and I don't doubt a minute but that your expertise on a sewing machine will get you the job—I would be living here alone," said Richard.

`"You might get married! I think I know someone who might have you," teased his sister.

With a very blank expression on his face, he replied, "I never thought of that! Well, Mom, I guess we'll just put this in God's hands and let him make that decision."

And they did.

Later that evening, Richard met Jalene at the gazebo. "You'll never guess what Mom dropped on us today at dinner," he said. "She has a newspaper from Middleton. There's a bridal shop up there advertising for a seamstress. That's my mother! She's an expert on a sewing machine and can make anything, even wedding dresses. She called the lady and plans to go work for them a few weeks to show them she can. Assuming she gets the job, she'll be living in Middleton. That would put me on my own again. Roseann said I could get married. What do you think of this?"

"I think," answered Jalene, "that we need to allow God to work this out. There is a place where you could live, Richard, if you don't want to live in a three-bedroom house by yourself."

"And where is that?" he asked.

"In the Bachelor's Barracks. It's on the side of the hill between the Cub House and the Manor. You can see the building from the lodge. It's where single guys live. Jimmy even issues a chow card for eating at a reduced price at the Cove, in case you choose to not do your own cooking."

"And here I was hoping you'd decide to get married and take care of me," pouted Richard.

"Well, my dear, God may do this for your mother to free you from your commitment, but he has not freed me. Besides, I am enjoying having Hester to take care of me. I have lived alone, too, remember? I'm not ready to give her up yet. I am learning a lot about cooking and preparing meals that just might come in handy someday."

"Even if I were to move from The Village, I'll wait until after Christmas. Mom and Roseann will need a place to come home to then," he said.

Taking his hand, Jalene led Richard down the path towards the lake and for a walk along the beach.

Jalene finished her lunch and went to pay for her meal. While waiting her turn at the cash register, she noticed it was still raining. By the number of folk in the Fisherman's Cove, she wasn't the only one who had opted to eat there rather than get out in the rain to go home for lunch.

A tall, slender man whose gray suit was somewhat dampened by the weather stepped inside the entrance, folded his umbrella, and looked around. He turned towards the exit as if to leave just as Jalene spoke to him.

"May I help you, sir?" she asked.

"I, I don't know. I ducked in here to get out of the rain. I didn't know this was a restaurant. I am looking for a man." He paused to get a paper from his inside coat pocket. "His name is Jimmy Hilton. I was told I could find him here. Do you know him?" he asked.

"Yes, sir," answered Jalene. "I'm Jalene Anderson. I work here. Just follow me and I'll take you to his office." She led the way to the elevator, punched M, and they rode up to the mezzanine. "Down there," she said, pointing, "is the front lobby and Market Lane for Lake Shore Resort. Jimmy's office is right here." Jalene knocked on the door.

A booming voice from within said, "Come in."

The tall man, still carrying his umbrella, entered the office.

Jimmy pushed himself to a standing position and put out his beefy hand. "I'm Jimmy Hilton. What can I do for you?"

Shaking Jimmy's huge paw, he said, "I'm Thomas Little. I'm a school teacher from the St. Louis area. I am on a search to learn who I am."

"How can I help you?" asked Jimmy.

Thomas looked at Jimmy a long moment. "I really don't know. I just hope you can. But it is a long story. Do you have time just now? I don't want to interrupt anything."

Jimmy leaned forward and studied the man intently. He said gently, "Mr. Little, have you had lunch?"

"No, sir, I just got here. I stepped inside a doorway to get out of the rain to discover I was in a restaurant. A nice young lady offered to show me to your office," said Thomas.

"Allow me to rectify that situation, please." Picking up the phone, Jimmy dialed a number and said, "Trish, I have a gentleman in my office who needs a guest room and lunch. Allow him to order in or escort him to and from the Cove, whichever he chooses. Thank you, Trish."

Turning back to Mr. Little, Jimmy said, "Trish will show you to a room where you can freshen up and relax. Give her your car key, and she'll have a valet park your car in the garage downstairs. You can have him bring your things from the car to your room. After you have eaten, I'll be happy to hear what you have to tell me."

"Thank you so much," Thomas said as he left with the maid.

After Mr. Little left with Trish, Jimmy called Bob Summers at the police station. "Bob, this is Jimmy Hilton."

"Whatcha need, my friend?" asked Bob.

"I need a credibility check on a man named Thomas

Little, a school teacher from the St. Louis area. Let me know ASAP what you learn, please. And thanks."

"Consider it done," replied Bob.

Moments later, Jimmy answered the phone. "Yes?"

"Bob Summers is on the line," stated his receptionist.

"Thank you. Hello, Bob," said Jimmy

"Jimmy, I don't know much. Found only one Thomas Little in St. Louis County. Born 10 February, 1921. Served in the Navy during WW II. School teacher. Missouri driver's license. Wife and two children. Owns his home. Registered as a Democrat. Member of NEA. No marks against him, not even a speeding ticket. Sounds like a fine US citizen."

"Thanks, Bob, that is what I needed to know."

"No problem, Jimmy. Anytime I can help, call me."

Jimmy's receptionist buzzed him later that afternoon. She said, "A Mr. Little is here to see you, Jimmy"

"Fine. Send him in."

Jimmy pushed himself out of his chair to meet Thomas Little at the door. "Do come in," he said. "I hope you had a good lunch."

"Yes, I did, thank you," said Thomas. "I feel much better, too, wearing dry clothes. I appreciate the chance to make the change."

"Let's sit over here where we can be comfortable while we talk," said Jimmy. He indicated a couch for Mr. Little while he pulled a straight chair near by for himself. "You said you are searching for your birth family."

"That's right. I was adopted when I was a baby. All these years, I've often wondered about my birth, but I was busy growing up and enjoying the life provided me by the Littles.

After World War II, I went to college, became a school teacher, got married, and had a family. I was a happy, busy person. But things changed three years ago. My wife died from cancer. My son finished high school and went off to college. My daughter and I kept going. It was a struggle, but she graduated from high school last May and has entered college. I decided then that I did not want to live alone in that house. I turned in my contract unsigned. I decided I would search for my beginnings."

"And what have you learned?" Jimmy inquired.

"Not much, really," replied Thomas. "I first went to the orphanage. Adoption records are closed to the public in Missouri. If I had a valid reason, I might obtain a court order to see my records. None of the present employees I saw gave me any encouragement there. None of them was employed there in the Twenties. They were all too young, so I left. I was stumped; didn't know where to go next. But as I was leaving the parking lot, I saw an old man picking up litter. I approached him to learn he had been picking up litter there for many years. He lived nearby and just did it voluntarily. I asked him if he knew any of the former employees who might still be living. He gave me the name of a woman who had been a supervisor in the Twenties or Thirties he could not remember which. So, I went hunting for a Hannah Woods.

"I went first to the library archives to check the old city directories. I found a Hannah Woods at an address near the orphanage. She wasn't living there anymore. I went to the court house to learn that Mrs. Woods was living at a different address when she sold that house. This new address was a unit apartment in a housing area for seniors, but she was not the present occupant. That lady said that Mrs. Woods was a resident at the Red Rock Nursing Home.

"I did find her!" Thomas continued. "She's a spry little old lady; very alert. She remembered me! The reason she gave for remembering me was because there were two of us. Her niece had lost a baby boy at birth, so she had talked her into adopting a baby boy. Her niece was Vera Carson. She said they had named their boy Robert. According to her, Robert Carson is my brother. Both her niece and her husband are gone. The last she knew of Robert, he was married and lived near Lake Mozarkia. I made inquiries in town at a place or two, but the name was not known. I looked in the phone book, but I did not find a Robert Carson. One man whom I asked said to inquire of Jimmy Hilton at Lake Shore Resort. He seemed to think you know more people around here than anyone. Does that name mean anything to you, sir?" Thomas asked.

Jimmy nodded his head sadly. "Yes, it does. I am truly sorry to be the one to tell you this, but Robert Carson drowned some time ago trying to rescue a child who fell off the excursion boat. He was an employee of mine at the time. His wife, Lydia, still lives in The Village. Their daughter is in college at Middleton."

"Middleton? My son and daughter are both at Middleton. Now isn't that something!"

Jimmy asked, "Would you like to converse with Lydia?"

"Yes, I would," said Thomas.

Jimmy reached for the phone. After checking his directory, he dialed a number. "Lydia, this is Jimmy. I have a gentleman in my office who would like to see you. I'll send James over for you, OK? See you soon." Then Jimmy made another call: "James, I need you to go for Lydia Carson, please. She knows you are coming. Bring her to my office, please. Thank you, James."

"Mr. Little," began Jimmy.

"Please, call me Thomas. I'm Mr. Little in the class-room."

"Well, Thomas, I think I can partially understand your feelings. I am a nobody; a child conceived out of wedlock. I was not wanted by my dad or my mother's parents. My dad was the town drunk. My growing-up years were miserable. I didn't discover who I really am until I met Jesus Christ and learned that he loved me enough to die for me on a cruel cross many years ago. After I invited God into my life, he made me a new person: I was born again! God has been my partner in this endeavor here at Lake Shore Resort. He has really blessed! I never married. My employees are my family. We have a caring community here. I've learned that it is not the name you bear but what you are inside that really counts. The name I am proud to bear is Christian. I hope you are in that family, too."

There was a light tap-tap on the door, and Jimmy boomed, "Come in."

Lydia stepped through the door. She smiled at Jimmy, took one look at Thomas Little and turned white as a sheet.

"R-R-Robert?" she questioned.

Thomas stood to his feet. "No, Mrs. Carson, I am not Robert. It does please me, though, if I favor him. I am Thomas Little. I was adopted as a baby. I am searching for my birth parents. I was told that Robert Carson might be my brother."

Jimmy had eased Lydia into a chair while Thomas was talking.

"You do look like Robert. He was tall, just a little heavier, is all. He never knew he had a brother. Too bad he didn't live to learn that. He said he always felt so incomplete. Are you older or younger than Robert? Are there other children?" she asked.

"I don't know about any others. I found a woman who worked at the orphanage. She said there were two of us. My birthday is February 10, 1921. Is that older or younger than Robert?" he asked.

"That's Robert's birthday! You must be twins! Lydia exclaimed.

"I never thought of that!" said Thomas. "When she said two of us, I just assumed brothers—two little boys from the same family."

"Did you say this woman's niece adopted Robert?" asked Lydia.

"Yes, her name is Hannah Woods. She is a resident at the Red Rock Nursing Home in St. Louis. Vera Carson was her niece."

"I knew Mrs. Carson, but she died before our daughter had a chance to know her as grandmother. Have you learned who your parents were?" asked Lydia.

"No, adoption records are closed records. They are not available for the public to see. With a court order, a living adoptee may be permitted to view his records. The court seems to be very reluctant to open records, usually ruling in favor of the confidentiality for birth parents. I personally think I have the right to know. Other children know who their parents are. Why should I be discriminated against?" asked Thomas.

"I don't know the answer to that. It does sound a bit unfair. Tell me, how long do you plan to stay here?" Lydia inquired. "I've some family pictures that you might like to see."

"Oh, I would like that!" agreed Thomas.

Jimmy immediately saw Lydia's problem since she lived alone. "Lydia," said Jimmy, "I think that is a great idea. Why don't you gather up those photos and such that you would like to show Mr. Little. I'll send James over in the morning to get you and them. You can use one of the parlors off of the lobby."

"Thank you, Jimmy. Happy to meet you, Mr. Little," she said as she was leaving.

Jimmy turned to Thomas. "According to what you said, Hannah Woods told you there were two of you. She explained about her niece adopting one little boy whom they named Robert. But tell me this, how did she know you are Robert's brother? How would she know that you are the man who grew from that other baby boy? Did I miss something?" asked Jimmy.

"No, you didn't miss it. I did! That thought had not hit me yet. How did she know that a man named Thomas Little was the twin of Robert Carson?" wondered Thomas.

"I see only one explanation," said Jimmy. "For some reason, she has kept track of you. She evidently gave you the information you related without a moment's hesitation."

"Yes, she did. Just like she had it on file, just waiting to present it as soon as I said my name. I need to go back to see that lady. I do have some pictures and such with me that I can show Mrs. Carson in the morning. Thank you so much, Jimmy. I'll allow you to get back to your own affairs. I surely do thank you," he said, shaking Jimmy's hand.

Chapter 16

Although it had rained much of the night, the rain tapered off before daylight. When James went to get Lydia, the clouds were well gone, the sun was shining, and the raindrops sparkled like diamonds.

Thomas Little was in the lobby at Lake Shore Resort, awaiting her arrival. He was still so excited about everything that he'd had trouble sleeping. And now, he was unable to sit while he waited.

As soon as Lydia came in with James carrying a suitcase, he went to meet them. "Good morning," he greeted her, realizing that Lydia was a lovely matron. She had a glad smile for him and seemed excited, too. He walked with her out of the main corridor of the lobby to where three rooms, like alcoves, were clustered off a stub hallway. Each had a motif of the area: Redbud, Dogwood, and Bluebird. Thomas had selected the Bluebird Room, as it was farther back and seemed more private.

James put down the suitcase, received expressions of thanks from Lydia, and departed.

Thomas and Lydia immediately began talking and sharing pictures. He had a few with him. They were both surprised how their children were so near the same ages. Thomas picked up a photo of Robert Carson in his navy uniform and reached for a similar photo of himself in navy blues. He put the two photos on the table side by side. "No doubt about it," he said, "we must be twin brothers." Robert had served as a medic, and Thomas had been aboard a destroyer. Had their paths ever crossed, they would not have known it. The pictures just proved their alikeness.

"Have you told your children yet?" asked Lydia.

"No, I waited until I had a chance to see your pictures. Since your daughter is also a student at Middleton, I've been trying to decide how to get them, and us, all together."

"There's a possibility that the girls may have met since they are both freshmen and living on the third floor at Rachel Hall. As for our getting together some time, why not plan to do that during their Christmas vacation?" she asked.

"But where?" Thomas asked. "My house in St. Louis would not accommodate all of us, and I'm sure your house here would not, either. I am open for suggestions."

"I'd say here at Lake Shore. This place is especially attractive at Christmastime. We all contribute to a beautiful display of the real meaning of Christmas. People from miles around come to see the lights that tell the story of Christmas. Your daughter could stay at my house. I have a sister who also lives in The Village. She has a son and a daughter. We could take her daughter, and you guys could all bunk with Richard, my nephew. How does that sound?" Lydia inquired.

"I think that sounds wonderful! You must have been thinking about our families having some time together, right?" he asked.

"Yes. I just feel these cousins need some free time together away from books, classes, and such. They need a time to get to know each other in an atmosphere of love and caring. That is the family aroma Jimmy instills in all of us here. We are one big family working together to help each other," she added.

"This is such a beautiful place. I was awestruck by the beauty of the morning. I stood on the balcony outside my room to watch the sun come up across the lake and break through the mist," said Thomas.

"You've only seen one little bit. There are acres and acres to this resort. There are footpaths, bridal paths, nature trails, parks, flower beds, and such everywhere you turn. And at every turn there is something beautiful—a vista of sky, water, and earth. God the Creator did a marvelous thing when he made this part of Missouri."

"That is one thing that amazes me so. I have lived all my life in St. Louis—except for World War II—and I never realized that such as this even existed. I'll be thrilled to introduce Mark and Karen to this place. I am sure it will be a lovely place, even in winter. I can almost picture those evergreens draped with snow."

Lydia laughed. "We do have snow, but not necessarily at Christmas."

"I do have one thing that I need to do," Thomas said.

"And what is that?" asked Lydia.

"Well, as Jimmy and I were visiting last evening, we realized that I need to go back to see Mrs. Hannah Woods. How did she know, when I told her my name, that I was the brother to the boy her niece had adopted? There must be an explanation as to why hearing my name triggered the right response. I must go see her as soon as I get back to St. Louis. I just hope I am not too late. She isn't young."

"I do hope you get to see her in time," Lydia said. "It saddens me that Robert did not get to know he had a brother. You are very much like him, even your voice. It's uncanny. But I do appreciate your sharing about your family, your wife, and her death. I'm sure she was a very special person. I'll call Sarah to tell her this news. She can look up her cousins on campus if she hasn't already met them. Then at Christmas, they can have a chance to be together. I am looking forward to that."

"So am I," agreed Thomas as he helped her place the items back into the suitcase. "I do appreciate your sharing with me about my brother. The manner of his death is extra proof that he must have been a fine person."

Thomas took the suitcase and walked with Lydia out to the lobby, where James was waiting for her. James took the suitcase and escorted Lydia out to the car.

Chapter 17

Hester was in the kitchen, getting out the ingredients needed to make pumpkin bread, when she heard a knock at the door. Answering, Hester was surprised to find Lydia Carson.

"Why, Lydia, what a happy surprise! How did you get here?" she asked, seeing no vehicle.

"I walked. It's such a crisp fall day, I decided to go for a walk. I hoped the fresh air would clear my head."

"Oh, do you have a problem?" asked Hester.

"Yes, I do. And I'm bothered, besides," she said, taking off her scarf and sweater. She sat on the couch and continued, "This may be news to you, but last September I met a man who had just learned he was Robert's brother. Robert knew he was adopted as a baby, but he did not know anything about his own family. This man—his name is Thomas Little—is not only Robert's brother, he is an identical twin. Hester, he told me about his children, his work, losing his wife to cancer, and I've told him about Robert, our family and such. He looks like Robert, sounds like Robert, and seems to be such a nice person."

"But what is the problem, Lydia?" asked Hester.

"Hester, I'm scared! I am drawn to him! It's like falling in love with Robert all over again! After he went back to St. Louis, Thomas went back to see the woman in the nursing home who had first told him he had a brother. She had said there were 'two of them.' He thought two brothers from the same family. He never once thought about having a twin. She said her niece, Vera Carson, had adopted the one and named him Robert. But Thomas wondered why when he said he was Thomas Little that just his name caused her to give out the information about Robert. He went back to see her and learned that she is his adopted grandmother. It was her daughter, Virginia Little, who adopted him. Thomas never knew he had any kind of grandmother living. Why do people keep these things secret?

"Anyway," she continued, "Thomas and I are planning to get our two families together over Christmas. I've talked with Richard, and he'll keep Thomas and his son Mark at his house. I'll take Roseann at my house. She can sleep with Sarah. I was wondering if you might be able to let Karen Little stay here with you?"

"Of course I can, Lydia. Jalene is going with her parents to Middleton to be with Karl and Janelle over Christmas. We have just learned that Janelle is expecting."

"How wonderful! I know they are thrilled!" Lydia added, "Hester, I need you to pray for me, please. Thomas calls me often. He's lonely, too. I think I might be falling in love with him. But I don't want to love a ghost. I do care for him. He's so easy to talk with and all that, but I am afraid. How can I know that what I feel is for him and not because he reminds me of Robert?" she asked.

"Of course I'll pray for you, Lydia. We'll just ask God to reveal this to you as a certainty since it affects the two of you and your families. We can begin right now." Taking Lydia's hand, Hester bowed her head and began to pray: "LORD, here we are, two lonely women. We so appreciate the comfort of your presence in our lives. We thank you for all you have provided for us: A place to live, our daily bread, and most of all, LORD, for your forgiveness. Do be with dear Lydia, LORD. Give her encouragement to do what pleases you. Give her discernment, LORD, to be certain about her feelings for Thomas Little. If this union is in your plan for her life, LORD, please allow her to recognize that. But if it is not, LORD, give her the grace and the courage to accept that, too. We love you, LORD, and thank you for your merciful kindness. In Jesus' name we pray. Amen"

"Thank you, Hester, I'll come again. Bye now."

Chapter 18

It had snowed the previous night. Hester had seen just a dusting on the trees when she first got up. But since the sun had come out, the snow had gone away.

Hester finished adding a can of mixed fruit to the strawberry gelatin, sprinkled coconut over the top, and placed the salad in the refrigerator. That, with the cookies I made yesterday will be our dessert when Jalene comes home for lunch, she thought. She had just tossed the empty can and wiped the countertop clean when she heard someone knock at the door. She quickly washed her hands. Drying them on her apron, Hester hurried to the door.

"Lydia!" she exclaimed, "how nice to see you again. Do come in."

"Good morning, Hester," said Lydia. "I hope I am not interrupting anything."

"No, no. I just finished a fruit salad for lunch. I'm ready to sit a spell." She invited Lydia to sit down.

"Hester, I think I have cabin fever. I'm about to go nuts being at home alone. It was bad enough when it was only Sarah and me, but I knew she would be coming home each day to spend the night. I had someone to cook for, to do laundry for," she paused, "you know. But that's not so now. Sarah is away, and I am alone. I don't want to cook. I don't want to clean house. I don't want to do anything. Sometimes I am so lonely I just cry. I miss Robert so much. Everything in the house reminds me of him. But I cannot afford to move. As long as I remain Robert's widow, I can live in The Village. Jimmy is providing me with a house with all utilities paid just because Robert's death was a result of his being Jimmy's employee. Hester, I have never worked away from home. I am just a homemaker and that's all."

"I know the feeling," agreed Hester, "but I also know that Jesus is the Good Shepherd, and I am one of his sheep. I know he provides for me and takes care of me. Lydia, have you ever claimed Jesus as your Savior and Shepherd?"

"Yes, but I don't seem to have the security you talk about," said Lydia.

Hester reached for her Bible. She also gave Lydia a sheet of paper and a pencil. "Let's read this together and you can write the phrases to personalize Psalm 23."

"The LORD is Lydia's shepherd.

"Lydia shall not want.

"He makes Lydia to lie down in green pastures.

"He leads Lydia beside the still waters.

"He restores Lydia's soul.

"He guides Lydia in paths of righteousness for his name's sake.

"Even though Lydia walks through the valley of the shadow of death, Lydia will fear no evil for you are with Lydia.

"Your rod and your staff comfort Lydia.

"You prepare a table before Lydia in the presence of Lydia's enemies.

"You anoint Lydia's head with oil.

"Lydia's cup overflows.

"Surely goodness and mercy will follow Lydia all the days of Lydia's life.

"And Lydia will dwell in the house of the LORD forever."

Hester spoke gently. "Lydia, if you know in your heart that Jesus Christ is your Savior, he is also your Shepherd. Trust him to care for you, to provide for you, and to lead you where you need to go. And remember, wherever that is, he is with you, even through the dark valley. Talk to him. Learn from him. Lean on his leadership. Trust him, Lydia. He loves you."

Hester asked, "Has Thomas declared his intentions yet? Or does he still call you?"

"He calls me often, not every night, however. He's lonely, too. We just talk and talk. We realize our children's feelings are a big concern. We think they are accepting the idea of being cousins. But nothing has been said about joining together as one family. I don't even know if that is what Thomas is thinking. And if he were to propose, I don't honestly know what I'd say."

"Is Thomas saved, Lydia? Is he a sheep? You cannot mix goats with sheep, you know," Hester said.

"I really don't know. He attends church but—"

Just then Hester's clock struck eleven. "Oh, my," exclaimed Lydia. "I need to go home! You have a noon meal to prepare! Thanks you for your prayers and concern, Hester. Bye."

Chapter 19

One afternoon in December, Jimmy answered his buzzer, "Yes?"

"Jimmy, a Thomas Little is here to see you," said his receptionist.

"Send him in, please."

Jimmy pushed himself out of his chair and went to open his office door to greet his visitor. Shaking hands with the tall man before him, Jimmy said, "What a nice surprise! Glad to see you, Thomas. Come in and have a seat. Are you just passing through, or will you spend the night with us?"

"I'm glad to see you, Jimmy," Thomas replied. "Yes, I am staying over night. No, I do not know my birth name yet. Like I told you over the phone, I did go see Hannah Woods again. She said Virginia Little was her daughter. I never knew Mom's mother was alive. What kind of rift would cause a mother and a daughter to sever all contact? 'Something is rotten in the state of Denmark.'"

"In my case, Thomas, my dad was a drunk from the wrong side of town. He was forced to marry my mother to give the baby a name. I know nothing about how they met or whether they had ever cared for each other. Her dad was a banker. I never even knew my mother's maiden name. Her dad disowned her; didn't give her a dime. My dad hated her dad with a passion. When he'd get drunk, he'd come home and take his anger out on her. I was overseas when he broke a whiskey bottle over her head then beat her to death. He hanged himself in his cell rather than face a murder trial. My mother had a nice house that she left to me. I sold it to buy land here on the lake. Maybe, some day, I can find out some of the facts. I've just never had any desire. My growing up years were awful. I prefer to forget them. But my example of a child conceived out of wedlock caused a rift in my mother's family. Economics may have entered in or even religion. Catholics, Jews, and Protestants were not to marry out of their own faith back then. I just haven't needed to know. I am too busy trying to make better things to happen," concluded Jimmy.

"You said when I was here before, that just knowing my family name was not all that important. In your eyes, being a child of God was what really counted. Would you elaborate on that idea?" asked Thomas.

"Well, Thomas, Jesus told a parable about a wealthy man who had two sons. The younger son asked for his inheritance, took it, and went to a far country. When he ran out of funds, all of his friends deserted him. He finally got a job feeding pigs. For a Jewish boy, that is getting low. It didn't make any difference that he was the son of a wealthy man. Nor did it matter that he knew how to dress well or how to conduct himself at social events. The fact was, he was broke and could not buy himself anything to eat. He had no marketable skills, so he had to take what job was available. Jesus related that the boy came to his senses. One day out in the pig pen, he realized that his dad's servants had plenty to eat and clean clothes to wear. So, he decided to go home, to throw himself on his dad's mercy, and to ask to be a servant, as he was no longer worthy to be called his son. He did go home. His father saw him a long way off, recognized his son, and ran to meet him. Dad had been watching for his return. He kissed his son and welcomed him home. Then they celebrated (Luke 15:11-32). Why? Because no matter where we have been or what we have done, the Heavenly Father is waiting for us to come home. If we confess our sins (sincerely repent of, and be sorry for our sins, and ask Him for forgiveness), he is faithful and just to forgive us our sins and to cleanse us from all unrighteousness (1 John 1:9). Now that is the family I am a part of! I gladly bear the name Christian and thankfully look towards my home in heaven with the LORD Jesus."

"You and Hester must be in the same family," Thomas said. "Lydia was so excited when I called her the other evening. Hester had her to write down a paraphrase of a Psalm they had studied together. Lydia told me she had rededicated her life to Jesus. Then she asked me if I were saved."

"Are you saved, Thomas?" asked Jimmy.

"I've attended church all my life. My folks had me christened when I was a baby. Since I was in the church, I just thought that was sufficient," he said.

"Thomas," Jimmy said gently, "I think you need some time to be alone with God's word. You will find a Bible in your room." Reaching into a drawer of his desk, Jimmy took out a small pamphlet and handed it to Thomas. "You take this with you. Read these scriptures and allow God's word to answer your questions. Take your time. I'll be right here if you wish to talk some more."

"Thanks, Jimmy, I'll do that. I need to know the truth." They shook hands again, and Thomas left Jimmy's office.

Chapter 20

Christmas Eve

Last evening when Hester washed the supper dishes, it was raining a soft, gentle rain. The temperature must have dropped in the night, as this morning the droplets were frozen on every limb and twig. The weight of the ice had caused the dead blooms on the mums to bend their heads. To Hester, the whole row of mums looked like a pew of folk with heads bowed in prayer. The ice on them sparkled like diamonds in the sunlight.

Hester was glad Charles, Ruth, and Jalene had left the day before for Middleton. That curving and hilly blacktop between here and there might be a bit dangerous if covered with a glaze of ice. She had prayed that the ones coming today from St. Louis would have a safe trip.

Tomorrow will be Christmas. Hester could not recall when Christmas had last fallen on Sunday. She just felt that made the day extra special. Jalene said the work force in the various departments had a choice—either Friday and Saturday off or Monday and Tuesday. Lake Shore Resort would be closed to the public on Christmas Day. This was widespread knowledge. Those guests who came from a distance to see the displays knew to leave no later than noon on the 24th. Jimmy wanted all of his employees to have the opportunity to be with their own families over Christmas.

Jalene had opted for Friday and Saturday to be off. She and her parents would spend Christmas with Karl and Janelle in Middleton. They would return Sunday afternoon, as Jalene needed to be at work on Monday.

Hester had put clean linens on the bed in Jalene's room to have it ready for company. She was first scheduled to have Karen Little as her house guest, but she might have Roseann instead. Karen had become so attracted to her new cousin, Sarah Carson, that she might feel more at ease at her house. Either girl would be fine with Hester.

Since the resort was closed, Lydia, Martha, and Hester had agreed to prepare the meals for the whole crew and take turns being hostess. This Saturday evening was Hester's turn. She felt she had everything under control. She had baked two fruit pies and made a chocolate sheet cake. She had a large gelatin salad and the makings for a garden salad in the refrigerator. She had the ham ready for the oven, as were the sweet potatoes. In addition, Jalene had made three kinds of candy to take to her sister but had fixed a pretty plate for Hester's company.

Hester had invited Jimmy to join them for the meal. He would make ten. She planned to put the five adults at the round oak table, the three girls at the card table against the wall, and fix places for the two young men at the kitchen table. It might be a little tight, but close fellowship never hurt anyone.

The coffee pot was ready to plug in, and she had two pitchers of tea (one sweetened) sitting in the refrigerator. Really, the only thing left to do was to make the dinner rolls.

Hester busied herself by putting a crochet tablecloth on

the round table. She put red tapers in a double candle holder and laid sprigs of evergreen around. She rolled the napkins to slip inside the Christmas napkin rings. She made a trip to her bedroom to look in her dresser for a white crochet scarf the right width to drape over the television set. On it, Hester placed the wooden stable and the wooden hand-crafted figures of her nativity set. With the TV screen covered, the nativity was the focal point.

She turned Uncle Will's chair sideways to allow more room for the card table she had borrowed from Martha. She pushed the table against the wall and placed three folding chairs at the table. She covered the table with a small cloth, put a single red taper in a holder, and added a sprig of evergreen.

Hester brought in her china and set the places. On her next trip she got the silverware chest. Very carefully she placed the knives, dinner forks, the salad forks, the teaspoons, the dessert forks, and the iced tea spoons in their places on the table. She put a set of salt and pepper shakers on each table and a butter knife. The sugar and creamer were on the big table where the adults would sit. She doubted if any of the others drank coffee yet.

Going back to the kitchen, she noticed the time and checked her bread dough. She washed her hands again, dried them, and then brushed her hands with flour. She punched down the bread, pinched off dough, made a ball, and placed three balls in each cup of the well-greased muffin pans. Hester had been making cloverleaf rolls since she was a girl. It was so routine that she chose this time to pray: "LORD, I thank you for the cooking skills you have given me. Thank you that I can have a part in this family gathering today. May each one who eats this bread be aware that you are the Bread of Life. Only through you can we have eternal life. Thank you, LORD, for sending your Son to be born in Bethlehem. Thank you that he paid for my sins on Calvary. And thank you, LORD, for his resurrection and mine, too, someday. LORD, grant the Little family a safe journey, and may you be honored by this day. Amen."

Sidewalks were dry and the air was crisp when Martha and Roseann came across the street to Hester's house about 4:00 that afternoon. Richard had gone in the car to get his Aunt Lydia and Sarah. Lydia gave him three balloons to blow up. He put one on the porch to Hester's house, and the other two he tied to the street sign. Lydia had told Thomas to follow the main drive through the resort onto Village Drive, and that she would mark their street and Hester's house with balloons.

Hester greeted her company and took their wraps to her bedroom to lay them on the bed. She returned to the living room in time to see others coming up the front walk. Hester opened the door to welcome the tall man and his two grown children. "Come in, come in," she said. "Welcome to my home. I am Hester Wirth."

"I'm Thomas Little, and this is Mark, and this is Karen."

Sarah had caught her breath when she first saw Thomas Little. Slowly she let it out and walked over to greet Karen. "So nice to see you again, Karen," she said. "Here, let me help you with your coat."

Karen turned to Thomas. "Dad, this is Sarah. I've told you about meeting her at Middleton."

When Thomas turned to speak to Sarah, he was speechless at first. He said, "Sarah, I am pleased to meet you. You remind me very much of a little girl who used to live across the street from us. She had pretty red hair, freckles, and two dimples."

That make Sarah smile, showing off her dimples. "Did she stomp her foot like this when she got mad?" asked Sarah, stomping her foot.

Thomas laughed. "I don't know, but she may have."

Meanwhile, Mark and Richard had paired off to get acquainted. Mark kept watching Roseann, who was helping Martha and Hester put food on the tables, thereby giving Lydia and Thomas opportunity to introduce their children. Richard caught Roseann's hand as she started back to the kitchen and said, "Mark, this is my sister, Roseann. She's a freshman at Middleton. You may have seen her on campus or in the library. She's such a bookworm that she may even have a bed there."

"No way, Richard," Roseann laughed. "My monitor knows every move I make. If I were not to check in, she'd call out the hounds to find me."

Mark noticed the camaraderie between this brother and sister. He also saw that Roseann was really a lovely young woman. He'd keep an eye on her.

Everyone knew when Hester took the rolls out of the oven. Just then there was a knock at the door.

"Who could that be?"

"I thought we were all here."

Hester went to the door to welcome Jimmy. "Come in, Jimmy, you are just in time." She took his topcoat to the bedroom. Coming back, Hester spoke to the assembly. "I want to welcome you to my home. 'Christ is the Head of this house, the Unseen Guest at every meal, and the Silent Listener to every conversation'. This is my friend, Jimmy Hilton. I have prepared places at this table for the five adults, the card table for the three girls, and the two young men there," she said, pointing to the other table. "Let us all join hands, please, to offer thanks for our food. Some of you are related because your mothers were sisters; some are related because your fathers were brothers; but we can all be related if we are God's redeemed children. Jimmy, would you express our thanks, please?"

"Father, we thank you for this day, for this special occasion, for this food, and especially for your Son, whose birth we celebrate. Accept our thanks, dear Father, and strengthen us to be your faithful servants. In Jesus name, we pray. Amen"

When they sat down, Sarah was careful to sit on the side where she could clearly see the adults at their table. She wanted to watch this man who looked so much like her dad and to observe how he acted with her mother. She knew her mother had experienced years of being alone without her beloved Robert. She figured Mr. Little (she had a hard time thinking of him as Thomas) was a lonely person, too. Could the desire for companionship be a strong enough bond on which to build a marriage? When Sarah got home the week before, she realized there was a new "aliveness" in her mother. She moved and did things with a purpose. She was animated and desirous of the days ahead. Sarah knew this weekend was the focus. Christmas? Yes, but not entirely. The cause was Thomas Little. She wondered, could I accept this man as the father figure in our home?

Mark and Richard went to the kitchen table, where Hester had set places for them. As Mark was in the lead, he went to the far side of the table which gave him the seat facing the others. He could see the adult table where the two sisters, Martha and Lydia, were sitting. Moving his chair just a little to the left, he could see the back of one girl at that table. It wasn't his sister, and she didn't have red hair, so it had to be Roseann's back he could see. He could tell there was a lot of chatter and laughter going on at the girls' table. Well, the girls were already acquainted and had much in common to talk about, he thought. I'll just visit with this guy and learn what I can about his sister.

Mark soon learned that Richard was easy to visit with as they related tidbits about their families. The name Jalene kept popping up in Richard's conversation, so Mark inquired, "Who is this Jalene?"

"She's the answer to my prayers!" said Richard. He told Mark about his experiences of the previous three years and how God had changed their jobs and moved their families just across the street from each other. He told about their love for each other, but they were having to wait about announcing any wedding plans. "You see, we had made other commitments before we found each other. We are not free to move forward with our plans until those are fulfilled. My mother obtained employment in Middleton and has become self-supporting, so I am free of mine. But Jalene still has a commitment to Hester. We shall just have to be patient and wait. In the meantime, Jalene is living here and learning from Hester about being a homemaker. In case you haven't noticed, Hester is an excellent cook." Richard added.

"Wow! And you think all these things happened because God is moving you around like pieces on a chessboard?" Mark asked.

"Do you know anything about sheep?" Richard asked.

"Not much. They're animals. They need food and water," answered Mark.

"That's true. They also need a shepherd. He is the one who leads them to find the pasture and water. Notice, I said lead.

Other animals are driven, but you cannot drive sheep. They are led. The sheep trust their shepherd to lead them where they need to go to find food and water. They trust the shepherd to keep them from predators," related Richard.

"That's interesting," Mark said, "but what has that to do with—"

"Mark," Richard said kindly, "those of us who are God's redeemed children are his sheep, and he is our Shepherd. We trust God to lead us for our best interests. We trust him, obey him, and just follow him wherever he leads. While Jalene and I are waiting, I am saving money to buy some rings. One of these days we can publicly announce our intentions."

Thomas Little stood up to speak to the group. "While these dear ladies are busy clearing the tables, getting ready to serve our dessert, I want to make a few remarks. Last September when I came to Lake Shore Resort, I was looking for a man named Jimmy Hilton. I had no idea I'd be involved in such a chain of events. It was raining that day, and just as I left my car, it began to really rain hard. I ducked into a doorway to get protection from the weather and found myself inside a restaurant. I was greeted by a young lady who willingly took me to this man's office.

"I had just learned one thing: I had a brother whose name was Robert Carson. This poster I have in my hand has on it pictures of two men who served in the U.S. Navy during World War II. One of them is Robert Carson, and the other is Thomas Little. They were mounted to prevent the temptation to look on the back." Thomas handed the poster to the three girls. Then he continued. "I found Robert's widow, and today I have met Robert's daughter. Lydia and I have talked and talked, shown family pictures to each other, and have found many mutual characteristics. I am so grateful for the warm welcome you have extended to me and my family. However, the search isn't over. I have yet to learn the name of the woman who gave birth to twin sons and what reason there was to place them up for adoption. Did she die in childbirth?

"Then today, I got another surprise: Sarah Carson. She is a lovely girl—fiery red hair, freckles—and she said she stomped her foot when she was little and wanted her own way. Lydia and Martha say there are no red-haired persons in the Underwood family. Did Sarah pick up that trait from her father's side of the house?

"In conversation with Jimmy, he told me that as important as it is to know your own name, there is another family name that has greater importance, and that's the name 'Christian.' I came back to Lake Shore Resort two weeks ago to see Jimmy Hilton again. We talked. He gave me some scriptures to read, and I went to my room. I did some serious Bible study and asked God to show me the truths I needed to know. I had been baptized as a baby into a church and felt that was enough. I attended church some and thought I was heaven-bound. I learned that was not God's plan. Heaven is his home. Only by following his plan through the blood of Jesus shed on the cross can anyone enter into his heaven. I learned we are all sinners, but I was a lost one. I wept, prayed, and God forgave me. Peace, sweet peace. I got it that day. I am still learning. I do not know what the future holds, but I am willing to allow God to be in control. Just wanted you to all know this. I'm not only happy to be a part of this family. I am also happy to be a part of God's redeemed family that Jimmy talks about." Turning to Lydia, Thomas said, "To answer your question, Lydia. Yes, I am saved." And Thomas sat down.

"Amen."

"Praise the LORD."

On a trip to the kitchen for more pieces of pie, Martha handed the pictures to Mark. He studied them carefully and passed them to Richard. "That is really uncanny. I've seen Dad's picture many times, but I cannot tell you which of those guys is my own father."

"They certainly do look alike," agreed Richard. "Aunt Lydia says they even sound alike. Uncle Robert was a fine man. I don't hardly remember him, but those who do speak highly of him. He was captain of an excursion boat here on the lake. He attempted to save a little girl who had fallen overboard. Sarah was quite small when she lost her father. I had just finished high school when I lost mine. No time is a good time to lose a parent. It's awful," said Richard.

"I know," agreed Mark. "I lost my mother before I finished my senior year. We really struggled. I know it was awful for Dad and Karen when I left for college."

"That must have been hard on you, too," agreed Richard.

"Karen and I had to do some quick growing up after Mom's death. There were so many things Mom did to keep the household running that we didn't realize until they weren't being done. Dad had it rough, too. He had to keep his mind on his job at school, grade papers, etc. He couldn't buckle, as we were all dependant upon his salary. I have a greater appreciation for my mother. I still miss her," added Mark.

"I know what you mean there. I still miss my dad. I learned a lot from him, but I still have things come to mind that I would like to ask him. But I wasn't like you, Mark. I didn't take the responsibility offered me. I ran away from home. I left my mother and sister to fend for themselves. Those were tough times for me. I even tried to forget God. But God used Jimmy Hilton and Jalene to get me back on track. By the way, what are you majoring in at Middleton?" asked Richard. "What do you plan to be?"

"I'm a quiet guy. I don't go out for sports and that kind of stuff. I enjoy books, working with numbers, and my music," said Mark. "My degree is in business, and I plan to be a CPA."

"That's Jalene's field! She works in the business office here at Lake Shore. You mentioned music—what kind?" asked Richard.

"I play the piano. My mother was a classical pianist. She started me on the piano when I was quite young. I'm studying now with Dr. de Kort at Middleton. I really like him."

"Mark, Karl de Kort's wife is Jalene's twin sister, Janelle. She is one of the librarians at Middleton. You have probably seen her in the library," said Richard.

"It's a small world!" exclaimed Mark.

"Maybe we need to move out of the kitchen, Mark, before they cover us with dirty dishes," said Richard.

They obtained their wraps from the bedroom. Richard picked up the folded table, while Mark and his dad got the chairs. They went across the street to the Nelson house.

"Mother may need these items at the brunch in the morning," Richard explained. "As soon as your sister joins us, Mark, I want to drive your family around the resort to show you the Christmas story in lights."

The ladies and girls finished the dishes and put everything away. Before they left, they each hugged Hester and thanked her for the delicious meal. They all agreed that they had had a happy time together.

Chapter 21

Hester slipped her nightgown over her head, added her robe, and returned to the living room. She needed to write in her journal the events of this day. Pulling up the arm on Uncle Will's chair, she wrote about all that had taken place. She was just finishing when the telephone rang.

Who would be calling at this hour of the night, she wondered as she picked up the phone. "Hello."

"Hester, this is Janelle. How are you? Tired, I'm sure."

"Yes, somewhat. We had such a good time. I was so glad to be included. How are you doing?"

"That's the reason I am calling, Hester. I have something I want you to consider. Please pray about this and let me know later. Okay?"

"Yes, of course. What is it you want me to pray about?" asked Hester.

"I hated to call as I know you have a houseguest, but I did need to let you be aware of this and—"

"But I don't have a guest," interrupted Hester. "The three girls wanted to be together. Sarah said she'd sleep with her mother and allow Karen and Roseann to have her bed. So I am alone. Take as long as you need."

"As you know, when I first learned I was to have a baby, I was sick for several weeks. We located a lady to help me keep house. Since she is a widow, she even agreed to just stay with me, which she did for several weeks. After I returned to work, Beth has been coming twice a week. Beth had told me that her daughter, Mary, was also expecting. When Beth went to her daughter's for Christmas, she learned that Mary had been put on complete bed rest until her delivery, which is sometime in March. Beth has gone to be with her daughter. I was wondering, Hester, if you would be willing to come live with us to be our caregiver. I know you are well qualified. Do pray about this, please, as I would love to have you."

"Of course I'll pray about this. I would be honored to be a helper in your home. Glad you thought of me. We shall see what the LORD has to say," agreed Hester.

"Thank you, Hester!" exclaimed Janelle. "I love you. Merry Christmas!"

Before Hester went to bed, she prayed: "LORD, Janelle needs some help. Am I to be the one? Show me, LORD, what I should do. Thank you so much for the happy events of this day, and especially for Thomas Little's salvation. I love you, LORD. Amen"

When Hester awoke on Christmas Day, she was met with a clean house and almost no evidence of the previous day's event. The china and silverware had all been put away. The crochet tablecloth was in the laundry. Only the red candles on the oak table and the nativity scene on the television indicated it was Christmas. All else was normal.

Hester fixed herself some breakfast. She opened her Bible to Luke to read while she ate her simple meal, but first she prayed: "LORD, here I am again and by myself. I do thank you for allowing me to be Jalene's companion these past months. It has been a delight to show her some cooking skills and some housekeeping shortcuts. Now Janelle needs some help. Lead me to know your will, please. I want to serve you wherever you want me to serve. I thank you for this day that we celebrate for the birth of my Savior. I thank you for your plan to provide eternal life through Jesus to all who will believe and trust in Jesus. LORD, I pray that Thomas Little's experience will have an effect on his children. May they also see their need of a Savior. I ask that you will be in the services today; that wherever the truths of your Son's birth is preached that you will bless. May those who do not know you see beyond the physical to recognize their need of a spiritual birth, to be born again. I am so grateful for that second birth. I know that I shall die physically one of these days, but I will not experience a spiritual death, as I am one of your sheep. LORD, I thank you for that. Forgive me, LORD. Show me what you want me to do. Amen."

Hester read the whole second chapter of Luke. Then she turned back to the Psalms. She stopped turning the pages at Psalm thirty-seven and read it through. "The desire of my heart, LORD, is to do your will," Hester prayed (Psalm 37:4).

Hester planned to attend the services at the chapel, but she was not going to be present at the brunch across the street. Since she was not a member of the family, she would not eat dinner with them later in the day, either. She was glad she could provide a place for them to gather the evening before. That was a blessing to her. Besides, Jalene would be coming home sometime that afternoon. They had some decisions to make, especially if she did go to live in Middleton for awhile.

That Monday, the day after Christmas, went slowly for Jalene. Being gone two days had stacked work on her desk. She really had to concentrate to keep her mind on the figures. What she wanted to do was to be with Richard, to tell him what she knew, and to hear about his weekend. At last, she filed the last piece and cleared her desk. (Jalene never left any papers on her desk overnight.) The day was over—finally.

She shrugged into her coat, hung her purse on her arm, and hurried home. As soon as dinner was over and she could graciously leave Hester, she went across the street to the Nelson house.

Martha answered her knock. "Do come in, Jalene. I have some friends here for you to meet." She led Jalene to the dining room, where the men were still sitting while they visited. "Sit down and join us," Martha said. "Would you like a piece of pie?"

"On, no, Martha, but thanks anyway. I was so eager to hear about your weekend I just couldn't wait any longer!" she exclaimed.

"Jalene," said Martha, "this is Thomas Little and his son Mark."

Richard had moved to stand behind Jalene's chair. Resting his hands on her shoulders, he said, "This is Jalene Anderson now. Someday soon, I hope, she'll become Mrs. Richard Nelson."

Thomas acknowledged the introduction, saying, "It's nice to meet you."

Mark said, "Wow! She does look like Mrs. de Kort!"

Richard explained, "Mark studies piano with Karl and is in the library a lot. He has seen Janelle but was not aware she was Dr. de Kort's wife. Oh, the girls are all over at Aunt Lydia's house: Mark's sister Karen, Roseann, and Sarah."

Mark added, "It's been an interesting weekend. I didn't know what to expect, but this has been different. I have met some very nice people. Even this place is different. I'd like to come back to see it in the summer. I imagine it is very pretty then."

Richard had walked to the coffee table, picked up the poster, and handed it to Jalene. "One of these pictures is of Thomas Little; the other is Aunt Lydia's picture of Uncle Robert. What do you think?" he asked.

After studying them a few moments, Jalene replied, "No doubt about it, these two men are identical twin brothers." Looking at Thomas, Jalene spoke to him. "I know that feeling, of being incomplete, but I knew why. I grew up knowing I had a twin. I looked for her in every crowd and on the streets. Everywhere I went where there were people, I kept looking. Now that you know, I hope that restless feeling will abate."

"So you and your twin did not grow up together?" asked Thomas, surprised.

"No, my mother took my sister out East to see Dad, who was hospitalized in Virginia. That was in November 1944 during World War II. Their train was involved in an accident in St. Louis during a blizzard. My mother was killed, but my sister was never found. Eighteen years later, we learned a young

German woman had found the crying child in the snow. She took care of her and raised her as her own. My grandmother, my aunt, and Hester raised me. Janelle was raised by Gretchen de Kort, Karl's aunt. God used Jimmy Hilton to give us a reunion two years ago. Hester believed Janelle was still alive and led us all to pray for her safe return. I hope I never forget the wonder and the thankfulness that I felt that moment I saw her for the first time. I wilted in the presence of God, who had answered our prayers. I felt so humble, yet I was grateful."

"God does wondrous things," agreed Thomas. "He used Jimmy Hilton to point me towards my Savior."

"God used Jimmy to send me back home to assume my responsibilities. He gave me a job that permitted us to live here in The Village," said Richard.

Martha turned towards Jalene. "I am in the process of buying a place in Middleton. Roseann can live with me next year. She already has work in the library. Between the two of us and her scholarship, we can take care of her college expenses. But what do you plan to do, Richard?"

Before Richard could answer his mother, Jalene said, "Oh, he can live in the Bachelor's Barracks until we can be married."

"Married!" exclaimed Richard. "When did you decide that?"

"As soon as Hester said she was going to Middleton," answered Jalene.

"Okay, out with it," stated Richard. "What do you know that we don't?"

"Janelle learned over Christmas that her live-in caregiver was no longer available. She called Hester to invite her to come live with them. Hester has prayed about this and feels God wants her to do this. She knows she'll be needed there until after the baby comes, and maybe longer. I can live alone. I've done that before. After we are married, Richard and I can have a two-bedroom house to share," she explained.

"That sound great to me!" exclaimed Richard.

With disbelief on his face, Mark said, "You mean to tell me that with one stroke of the brush, the whole picture is completed? Just like that!" He snapped his fingers.

"You might say so," agreed Richard. "If God sends Hester to Janelle, Jalene will have finished her commitment to Hester. My mother's move ends mine for this house. If that is what develops, then Jalene and I are free agents and could start our lives together."

Jalene added, "Janelle and Karl were married in the chapel here at Lake Shore just two years ago. That would be the natural place for our wedding, don't you think? And Richard, in case you have not remembered, my dad owns the jewelry store in Mozarkia. He might have some rings in stock."

After the laughter, they all congratulated the couple. Then Richard said, "Before we leave, I would like for you to join Jalene and me in prayer." The group held hands around the table while he prayed. "LORD, Jalene and I, with these friends, come today to thank you for the many things you have done these past several months to bring us together. We thank you for the love we share. We know that true love, abiding love, comes from you, and we thank you we can be responsible for a pinch of it. Thank you for our families, their support, and their willingness to pray for us. Bless them all. And LORD, grant that the home we plan to establish will be a blessing to your holy name. May we always follow like obedient sheep. We ask that you bless these new friends. Grant them safety as they travel home. And may you always have a place of leadership in our lives. We love you, LORD. Forgive us and use us. We pray in Jesus' name. Amen"

Meanwhile, across the street, Hester had finished the dishes, written in her journal, and was sitting with her Bible in her lap. She opened it to the book of Ruth and read all four chapters. "LORD," she prayed, "sometimes I feel like Ruth traveling to a strange new place. Just be with me and help me to be useful. Other times, I feel like an aged Naomi. She did get to hold her grandson, LORD. The nearest I can come to that is to hold Janelle's and Jalene's children. I pray that Janelle's baby with be healthy and will develop in favor with God and man. I pray for Jalene and Richard; that their marriage will have your blessings. Whatever you have planned for me, I want to do it. Just give this old body the strength. The desire of my heart, LORD, is to do your will. I love you. Amen."

Epilogue

Martha Nelson did move to Middleton, and Hester did go to live with Janelle and Karl de Kort. Lena Louise de Kort was born on the 21 of June, 1967.

Richard Nelson and Jalene Anderson were married in the chapel of Lake Shore Resort on the 18 of August, 1967. Jalene, like her sister Janelle, wore her mother's wedding dress. Jalene's attendants were Janelle de Kort and Roseann Nelson. Richard's groomsmen were Karl de Kort and Mark Little.

The reception, held in the lodge, was given by Charles Anderson, father of the bride, and his wife, Ruth.

Richard and Jalene Nelson now live on Woodfern Lane, Lake Shore Resort.